# THE GHOSTS OF SLAVERY'S DANCE: NO MORE CHAINS

# A. R. LEONARD

*"I'm pretty sure a scholarly journal wouldn't use my stuff."*
*Ha-ha! ~Nita Nae~*

Author's note: Discussions and scenarios in this book depict real life situations. Vieux Carre' & Black Codes were real for the time period depicted. Characters, names, and incidents mentioned are products of the author's imagination or are used fictitiously. Any resemblance to actual events or locales or persons, living or dead, is entirely coincidental.

All Rights Reserved © 2024 – Arnita R. Brown
Printed in the United States of America.
Imprint: Nita Nae's Books
Publishing & Distribution Company: Lulu.com

**ISBN: 979-8-9923146-2-5**

A. R. Leonard
***The Ghosts of Slavery's Dance: No More Chains ©2024***
Nita Nae's Books – Truthful Imagination © 2015
4859 W. Slauson Avenue, Ste. A - #354
Los Angeles, CA 90056

# The Ghosts of Slavery's Dance

## No More Chains

# Available

Amethyst in Love, (Amazon Kindle, 2019, Rev. 2025)

Unconditional Counsel (Lulu.com, 2020, Rev. 2025)

Apocalyptic 7 – Salvations' Cry (Lulu.com, 2021, Rev. 2025)

Embrace the Dawn to Live Again (Amazon.com, 2024)

Det. Brenda Sayers: Mercy Undercover (Lulu.com, 2025

# Future Books

Unconditional Counsel 2 – Fate Unbroken! (WIP)

Apocalyptic 12—Angels of Heaven's Armies (WIP)

The Container (WIP)

Opposing Fruit (WIP)

The Heart of an Untold Legacy: A Father's Story (WIP)

# Dedications & Acknowledgments

To God be the glory for all He has done in my life. I thank God for trusting me with this gift and allowing me to pay it forward for others to walk this path and journey as I learn to navigate these waters called writing and publishing. I never thought I would in this place of… Truthful Imagination.

To the servant that died, suffered, survived, and passed on their legacy through lineage, history, stories, and victories. I salute you as part of Your heritage.

God created all of us for a purpose, reason, and time.
*"Create, live, love, and be beyond our existence." ~Nita Nae*

# Introduction

*The Ghosts of Slavery's Dance*: *No More Chains*, is a Historical Romance. I wrote this book from a dream I had while writing *Unconditional Counsel*. I also remembered a scene from 12 Years A Slave, where the African woman was the lady of the house to a Caucasian man. This scene intrigued me to where I wanted to write from the African woman's perspective. I consider the significance of all the dreams I've had over the years, especially those I've remembered vividly.

I acknowledge every person taken from their home. I acknowledge the pain, hurt, and disgrace the actions of those on both sides: the sellers from Africa tribes, and those taken by slave traders cause. God had a purpose, a plan, and a reason for it all. I thank all the human beings that survived, endured, and loved despite the atrocities done to them. They are the reason behind this story.

# Contents

# Prologue

*"If there is no enemy within, no enemy outside can do you no harm." Les Brown (Negative People, 2015)*

Nakida

"Slaves have a story to tell. Millions will never have the chance. Death by hanging, lynching and other designs of bloody torture used, prevents them from doing so. My great-grandmother is the sole survivor of her people in America. She was the last one in my family to be a slave and still alive to recount her history."

Nakdi

"If not for my great-granddaughter craving to learn her history. I may have taken my story to the grave like so many others. The kids nowadays don't ask about their history, but Nakida convinced me otherwise. To relive it again was a tough decision to make. Slavery was a horrible existence. I experienced the harm and misery that it caused. For those being taken from the Motherland, the tribes who lost their loved ones, and those left behind with the guilt and the unknown. Yes! There were tribes who surrendered their people for a price, never forgiving such atrocity—betrayal. I didn't understand what happened to me and didn't know why until my later years of life. The outcome of my experience has been one of survival and triumph."

Nakida

"The rationale of what bondage is and the devastation it produced is nothing the history textbooks can tell us. Misinformation and thievery of Our Story could never provide those that came after them—truth. I perceive with time the correct knowledge will get out and teach our legacy for what it was and will be. Can it ever express the anguish and utter horror of what the slave man or women was going through? The intimate moments or grief in his or her own words? The slave acknowledges the stories read over the generations, as my great-grandmother acknowledges. Grateful, unlike most, to hear my great-grandmother tell me hers."

Our History and Mine:

Slavery has existed a long time. The Bible even talks about slavery, but the *Ghosts* corrupted what God had designed. The only cause suggested in the Pentateuch for selling a man into bondage without his consent: per the Jewish Encyclopedia is his inability to make due restoration for goods stolen (Ex. 22: 2), but from II Kings 4:1-7, in the kingdom of Israel the sons of an insolvent deceased debtor were sold for the father's debts, and from Isa. 4: 1, that in the kingdom of Judah the debtor was forced to sell his children to appease his creditors. The Law, unless the passage in Leviticus which speaks of "your brother," when he "waxes poor" and "is sold to you," refers to a sale for debt or the critics are right in ascribing to the laws has now found a later origin than that of Elisha or Deuteron-Isaiah, this is not supporting their usage of slaves.

*WE OWED GOD, BUT WE OWED AMERICA NOTHING!*

According to the Hebrew dictionary, a typical textbook answer means, "a shadowing forth, a phantom, a sketch, an outline." It gives the outlook that humanity is not as great as we think we are. But further researching this word, gives a more complete definition that means, "Whatever makes up humanity is remarkable or deserves respect." The Berean Newsletter, Daily Verse and Comment says,

"Though we are remarkable, we are an outline, a mere copy or representation. We are illusory compared to God because He is the reality."

Nakdi

In exploration of our faith, can we deny everything happens for a reason or being taken was not in God's Plan? There was no debt owed to America from the African, but none the less, there was a plan of promise: the plan of salvation. The Ghosts of Slavery's Dance never thought we'd become a great nation! We have survived, excelled, conquered, but we must never forget where we come from and why we must remember our sin and disobedience toward to the true and living God. As we can see today, there are generations who have forgotten God, their history, and where they come from.

For a vessel sailing the west coast of Africa, the mouth of the Senegal river offers the first refreshing welcome after the parched territory of the western Sahara. Further south, around the difficult promontory of Cape Verde, is the even more enticing estuary of the Gambia. Here the channel is broad—deep, carrying even modern ocean-going vessels as far as 150 miles inland.

"Gambia, where for me it all began—my journey."

From when Europeans explored these regions in the 15th century, these two great rivers attracted their attention. For a century and more, the Portuguese have them to themselves. They reach the Senegal in 1444 and the Gambia in 1455. In the 17th century the French and the British, by now imperial rivals, develop an interest in the two rivers. The French set up a trading station at the mouth of the Senegal in 1638. In 1659, they move it to St Louis, a more secure island. In 1677, they seize (from the Dutch) the island of Gorée, little more than a large rock off Cape Verde, but of immense value as a defensible trading station at this pivotal point on the coast. Meanwhile, the British concentrated their efforts on the Gambia. In 1661, Fort James is built on seventeen miles upstream. In the 1680s, the French send a detachment from Gorée to establish a provocative settlement at Albreda on the north bank of the river opposite Fort James. On the verge of a century and a half warfare against each other, France and Britain fortified settlements in Africa as they change hands between the two nations during the 18th century. The result, by the mid-19th century, is that Britain is the established European power on the Gambia, with the valuable addition of Bathurst (now known as Banjul). They use this island in the river's mouth from 1816 as a base against the slave trade. Balancing this, France has the Senegal and the important outpost of Gorée between the two rivers. The French were much more ambitious than the British in pressing inland. They establish a station at Médine, far up Senegal, in the 1850s. In 1883, a French expedition reaches Bamako on the Niger. They outflank the British, who restrict their interests to the banks of the Gambia. Thus, when the scramble for Africa begins in 1884, the British are at a disadvantage. When boundaries are agreed upon between the two nations, in 1889, Britain secures only a narrow strip along each bank of the Gambia. The French Senegal surrounded this territory. (Philip D. Curtin's book, *The Atlantic Slave Trade*, (1969), p. 221.)

Nakdi

Here is where my history starts.

# 1

## Knowing Her Intimately

In awe of my great-grand mother Nana's age, that's what I called her. Even more so, I was in awe that I was twenty-one and she was a hundred and four years old and still in her right mind to remember everything and how she told me she survived her ordeal of being one of the forcibly taken from her home in Africa (how she put it). My great grandma was born in 1836, and although, her journey was six years prior to the last slavery boats journey to the America's, her experience was familiar to the slaves before and after, but her ending was not the typical nuance.

I had heard the stories through my studies at Dillard University (formerly, New Orleans University). I never quite thought I could get a live record of what happened during slavery time or that my interest would be peaked to write about it. Although slavery had been abolished on paper, there was still this tumultuous way of life—the white colonists against everyone else. I still had to abide by the rules of having our own toilets, water fountains and places that only the colored folk could eat at. Because I had grown up in this era, I knew nothing else, but because of my great grandma paying for my education, there was nothing else to do but learn, and learn who I was as a human being.

My Nana was yet taller than most women, a little bent over, but spry and healthy. I could still count on her to be there for me. I loved my Nana, but what she was about to tell me, made me angry. It opened my eyes to the true hatred that still exists even now. It made me understand who I was, where I came from, and my identity as a woman of color—a human being period. I loved her more for surviving it all, and because I knew who she was inside. Her struggles, the decisions she made and never regretting her survival or the love she allowed to enter her heart was all I could do to be proud. My Nana could be bitter and broken. She could have a hatred in her heart for those that did not look like her. That was not her story. She understood what it cost the African. What it cost her personally as an individual from the hands of others that didn't look like her and from those who did.

"Momma, why did you never talk about the past and great grandma's history?" I had to ask one day.

"Nakida, I think it's because it's been a painful journey for even me. Your father and I live in constant worry, that one day, you too will have to experience what it was like up close and personal. We didn't grow up as slaves, but we lived in a time where our lives only meant something precious to us. Growing up, grandma paid for our education as well, but for us it seemed, like what's the point of it all. We had a different attitude about education and living here, at least I did. It was for our future survival and not just to get a job. We lived to survive and everything else was secondary. It's different for you and the generation you are in. Although, bigotry and racism is still rampant, you all are a little freer than we were," my mother Mary said.

"Will we ever be free of bigotry and racism?" I asked.

"Honestly, I don't know the answer to that question. I can only hope and pray for a time such as that, but to know the inner evil of one's heart can only be changed by the one who created them. Things can change at any moment. Maybe better laws can be passed, and people can finally stand up for what's right, but can the heart change? Will the people who believe they are better than everyone else ever change their hearts to embrace all humans?"

~

This in my great-grandma's words: "Run Nakdi!" Now six-years-old and having fun with the sisters away from our parents. I ran faster than them. One day, I was running and not looking in front of me. As soon as I turned, splat, I ran into the brown bark tree. Knocked unconscious for only a minute, my sisters as I woke were crying and shaking me. Getting to my feet, they felt relieved that they didn't have to run back to get our parents. As soon as they felt better, they laughed—we laughed so hard. It was a magical moment of sisterhood through fear of possible loss. We were together for now. Deciding to walk back to our village instead of running back, our togetherness was intact.

Bustling with motion, our elders talked, and our mothers cleaned and cooked what our father's killed for the day. Heat and steam rising from the pots of goodness. Brown dirt dusting our feet as we ran around our huts. That quiet stillness of the moment, us looking at each other and then continuing to run around as free bird of prey. Flowers that kissed the sun each day or misted as the rain falls upon us. Jumping at the sound of our name, we walked slowly to our mother as she hands us the baskets to take inside. Knowing nothing else but freedom and our families, living was not a struggle for us. We loved and lived for each other. Living to love others, to accept a mate one day, to be what our mothers and fathers taught us to be. We existed in the realm of our ancestry, our traditions, our village—our life.

My parents were hard working and kept a tight rein on us all. He was an important—respected person in our village. Taller than most of the men with dark smooth skin, a fierce warrior and hunter. I too wanted to be like him—more so than my mother. He had not become an elder, but they listened to his opinions. He would be an elder one day, we were sure of it. My mother was common to those around her with dark brown skin and catlike eyes, which were dark brown as well. Fierce in our common way, she taught us everything to survive. How to be a woman and fight for your own identity in the quietness of our serenity. Our families were close and unwavering in taking care of each other until the invasion and a surprise raid on our village happened.

~

I met Master Ben when he was close to twenty-one. He had established himself as a force to be reckoned with, even at that early age. He had red hair and olive skin. His parents had owned the Henderson Plantation for over 35 years and I had been one of the first ones brought there under Master Ben's command. I had been born in Africa, Senegal-Gambia, and yes, our Chief sold us out to save his own skin and his families. Even in that trying circumstance, I knew it had to be this way, it had to be me—chosen. My village was deep in the shadows of the trees. You couldn't just get there from the big water. The rivers flowed full of life and wealth for the Creator saw fit for us to be free. Many years of my life, I had never seen them, but I had heard about them and for that many years we were safe from the *ghosts*.

A day came like no other. There was panic and chaos, but I never fought them to get free, nor did I fight to get anyone else free. It's easy to say that I would rather die than to be taken. When your instinct and desire is to live, that's what kicks in. Seeing some of my village fight back and lose their lives by gunfire. I wondered what would have happened if I had made that choice to fight, but I didn't. In certain cases, it was best for them. God knew the reason.

On the Majestic, was the first time I had ever seen water so big— never ending. It seemed like with every wave. It swallowed me whole. I wasn't afraid to die, but I wanted to live more, and floated to the ship as if it was my life's destiny. It wasn't until I saw the ship up close and personal, that I felt fear. It was hard mentally and physically to be on that boat of torture for weeks and not truly understand the nature of my plight or the man lying next to me dead after weeks on the water. The stench of death and the rotting flesh made you wish you had died along with them or made you feel like you should have died in the fight to get free. Their bodies dumped out to sea for the flesh to be eaten. Their bones to create unmarked, watery graves at the bottom of the ocean.

It was like heaven coming down to visit me, when allowed to go on top of the ship. Only to be frightened at the ghost faces that would yell at me for no reason, other than to yell and be evil. Not moving much, I gazed blindly into the sun or welcomed the sprits of salt water from the side of the ship.

~

My great-grandmother paused to take a breath. She was all gray, a pearly white gray now and just as beautiful as when she had left Africa. She hadn't completely lost her accent, but you could tell life had changed her into who she would become. She was a cream espresso of loveliness and because I had never reached her height, I always had to look up at her.

~

"Let me back up a bit, Nakida." When we were finally going to be put on the ship, there was no amount of time to prepare for something that you had never seen or been on before. I screamed in horror as they were about to put me on a smaller boat to get the larger ship. The mean ole ghost man with the blonde scraggly beard and hair, and speckled face hit me hard with a stick. I started to suffocate. I couldn't move and crunched over in agony of not just the physical, but the mental. As I stood there in silence breathing hard. Tears stream down and I'm terrified to not make a sound— stuck in time. As soon as I could catch my breath, he was about to hit me again. When he raised his hand to strike me, this time in the face, the hand that was about to hit me again was stopped. I saw Master Ben for the first time up close and personally.

"If I am owner of these slaves, you will never hit one on my watch. We must get them home in one piece and I don't need you damaging them before we get there. Besides, I'm sure my father would not be pleased to know you are destroying his property and profit." Master Ben got close to his face, "Do you get my meaning Mr. Drexel?"

"Yes, Sir. I get your meaning loud and clear."

Of course, there was venom coming out of his veins, but he sure didn't want his pay taken away for one of the darkies dying by his hand. Before Master Ben left, he checked my stomach and my mouth to make sure there was no blood and then he walked away. I never made another sound.

Being on that ship was just like the other stories had been told before. The smell and the hot stench of death was toxic. They would every other day take us up to walk around and of course, they never let us out the chains unless one of us was dead or too sick to recover. There was a dead body dropped overboard every other day. Some would stop eating and starve themselves to death. Some got sick with disease and others died of a broken spirit and mind.

Most of us survived just to get where we were going and none of us knew where we would end up, but we wanted to live, nonetheless. Our eyes hurt, because the last few days before our arrival, we were not allowed to go up top, unless we were deceased. When we did finally get off the ship, it took about ten minutes for our eyes to adjust. Our bodies ached beyond measure. The pain of walking shackled and them tearing through our flesh to sometimes the bone was like being beaten five hundred times with a block of wood, but we were alive, and the pain reminded us of that fact.

We had no clue as to what would be done with us or to us. We were in a strange place, but I knew I had to be there, if nobody else did. I was already eighteen and fully developed in every aspect of the word. They lined us up like cattle outside the ship and Master Ben chose those he wanted to take home with him and the others would be sold off like a piece of meat, property, we were expressed to be—elsewhere. Master Ben stood twenty feet or so away from us and glared at each one as though we were nothing, but something at the same time. He rode off on a horse and returned twenty minutes later with his father in tow in a wagon. Money was all Ben's daddy cared about and a reason to torture us was in the minds of the rest of them ghosts.

As he scanned down the line, I watched every move Master Ben made as a bobcat stalking its prey. When he got to me, it was as if his eyes pierced mine and he stopped at me and did not look any further. I was not the typical looking African girl. Even my parents were somewhat ashamed of me for this aspect, even though it was hereditary from my father. They could not understand why I was taller than everyone else or why my skin wasn't as dark, but like I told them all the time, this is the way God made me and there was nothing I could do about it.

For a long time, I was ashamed of my parents' shame towards me. I was uncommonly strong in how I felt about myself and the people that called themselves family. I was six feet, one-inch-tall and I towered over most of the men in my village and the ones that were standing in line with me. Master Ben looked me up and down and decided I would be going with him. Why? I wouldn't find out until later. I wasn't sure what to think about it, but he had kept that other ghost from hitting me again and I was thankful for that much.

The harbor smelled like bodies and fish, but mostly bodies, with birds flying all around us and the clouds hovered over them. The clay ground made sure the dust was everywhere. It was a loud, bustling place. The bell ringing at a church always made me wonder why it was there. Sometimes the chains rang louder, especially when they made us run or trot like their horses on the buggy, but now the bell represented a new batch of Africans had arrived. The ghosts walked by looking and starring and the ghost children did the same. Long dresses from their necks on down to the ground, but they didn't all smell so nice either. I stood there wondering, pondering the absence of my language. The French influence was strong in that place. My ears hurt to hear them, so I had to tune them out to stay sane.

The other ghosts which is what I had decided to call them unshackled our arms but kept us tide together by chaining our waist and ankles. I could not speak their language, nor could they understand mine, but as Ben passed down the line, I put my hand on his chest to thank him for keeping the man from hitting me again. Another ghost came up behind Master Ben and hit me upside my head and I fell to the ground unconscious this time.

Unaware of what took place after, I woke up on a dirt-colored cushiony mat with a line of dry crusted blood running down the side of my face. Ready to kill at that point, I had forgotten for a moment my reality. I saw Master Ben come over to my bedside to see how I was doing. I liked him, but I didn't trust him. I didn't trust him because of what they had done to me and he was a ghost just like them. I didn't trust him because he didn't look like me. The irony of it all was that now, I had no one to trust but myself.

It was a shack with the sunlight flowing through the slits of wood on the walls. My head hurt, and I put my hands on my head to see if it would stop the pain. The blood was no longer dripping but the pain was still present and so was a lump. The shackles around me were no more. The maroon color stained my fingers. I get angry all over again. I wiped the blood with both my hands and wear it proud as war paint on my cheek bones. I screamed at the top of my lungs because at that moment, I knew that life for me was no longer in freedom. All I could see was the red and light through my eyelids. I scooted back on the mat and wanted no one near me. I kept my eyes closed until I could calm down.

My great grandma looked at me and said, "Would you have trusted anyone?"

"No Nana, I don't think I would have trusted anyone at that point either. To be honest, I don't know if I would have wanted to get off that ship alive." I said.

"Well, I guess you might not have been born had I not gotten off that ship alive."

"That's very true. I guess I really didn't think about it that way. The thought of none of us existing if you hadn't."

"Well, child, I think that's the reason I'm telling you this story in the first place, so you know where you come from and the history of your family. Let me get back to the story before I get too tired."

I looked down for a second to make sure that I had enough paper to write down as many notes as I could muster. "Okay Nana, please keep going." I could tell that she was getting ready to start as she sat back in her seat and closed her eyes.

# 2

## Meeting Beta

I looked around the room in that shack and I saw her standing there. She came close to me as Master Ben got up and went to the door to see what the commotion was all about outside.

"You need to be careful wit Master Ben. He's nicer than most, but he can tear the skin off you, if you cross him in anyway."

Her voice was the only other that could speak my language. I stayed silent because I didn't want her to know I could understand her.

After coming back from outside, he brought water. He handed it to me personally. As much as Beta warned me about him, I wasn't scared of him and nobody else. I knew that they could do all kinds of things to me, but I wasn't scared of them.

Oh, yes, let me introduce you to Beta. Beta was from our next-door village. I didn't know her, and she was five years older than me. I'll tell you more about her later.

~

My Nana livened up when she talked about Beta. The excitement in her voice was unmistakably loving.

~

He sat at the foot of the bed and I moved my legs as to not touch him. He moved in a little closer to me and Beta cringed and turned her head as though she knew what was coming. Like at any moment she was going to drop dead of fright. I moved in closer to him and slowly put my hand up to his face. I touched it to see if the non-pigmented skin would come off or if I could add some of my color to him like ceremonial paint. He was sweating like a bucket of water was just poured on him. The heat was sweltering and humid. I had decided to do to Master Ben what those other ghost men had done to me as we were lined up outside the little boat. I stuck my fingers in his mouth to understand what they were doing to me. What was the purpose any ole way? He snapped his teeth at my fingers as I pulled away. Within myself, I wanted to punch him, but the look on my face changed when he started to laugh at me and then so did Beta out of fear. I guess I didn't know any better, so I started laughing too. Belting it out just like they were. Mimicking their gestures.

Ben got up off the bed and Beta immediately jumped back out of her boots. He told her to take care of me for two days and prepare me for the house. After he left, Beta came to me and explained what he said. Beta was sure to follow Master Ben's instructions, because she was terrified of them all. I didn't find out why until many years later, but that's when I finally spoke to her and let her know that I understood what she was saying.

Not used to being waited on hand and foot, it was just not my way and after two days, I just couldn't take it anymore. I left to go outside and into the big house. Beta never saw me leave. She had been working in the field. I walked up the front steps and right through the front door. None of the others like me tried to stop me. I don't know if it was out of fear that they didn't say anything, they were in shock or they wanted me to be taught a lesson. As much as we all were in the same boat of slavery, some of us did think on those lines to help each other.

When I slowly, curiously walked through the door, the misses of the house screamed so loud, she could have woken up the dead. I didn't know to run, I just stood there looking at the ghost woman scream. Mr. Henderson came running down the stairs and Master

Ben came running through the back entrance. They all looked at me as though I was supposed to know I didn't belong there.

"Ben, what is the meaning of this? Why is this nigga gal in my Foyer?

As the misses was speaking to Master Ben in their own language, she slowly moved toward where Mr. Henderson was standing on the stairs. Master Ben put his hand up to me, but I didn't grab it. "Mother, this is one of the new slave gals that I just brought back. She doesn't understand our language or her place just yet. You all just go on back upstairs and I'll take care of her."

Master Ben just kept staring as though I was something he'd never seen before. I had not been the only African girl that had been brought there. Why was his look so curious? Maybe, he could sense the freedom in me and at that moment decided not to break it. The Henderson's walked back up the stairs indignant at their sons' response and spat out words of unconscionable disgust. He then turned from me to them to watch them go, but my still scarred head turned to see a place in the house that I had never seen before. None of it I had seen before. They were skinny and shiny, and the room was bright with the sun beaming through white crossed windows. The walls were lined with them, but there was only some that caught my eye. I had walked away by the time he turned to notice that I was no longer standing in front of him. I walked through the white colored wood and I could feel Master Ben watching me finally and following behind me, but I didn't care.

At that moment, I was afraid to touch anything, because I didn't want anyone screaming. My curiosity got the better of me and my hands magnetically move to grab it, but he grabbed it before I could touch it. He was speaking his language, but I couldn't understand him. I looked at him as if he could understand my body-language and it was saying, 'haven't you figured it out yet, I can't understand you. Why do you keep trying to talk to me in your language?'

Looking me square in my face as though he was trying to see into my soul. He looks down at the book that I was eyeing and opened it. Beta came running through the white wood, out of breath and terrified. She spoke to Master Ben as I stood there and then came and grabbed my arm to pull me out of there. I didn't want to leave that room, but I didn't want to cause any trouble for Beta. He smiled at me as though I was a child. In that moment in time, I had been his child. Master Ben seemed to want to protect me as soon as he laid eyes on me.

Beta was small, but strong. She pulled me all the way back to that shack they called a house. Once we walked through the wood, she slammed it behind us. Beta was angry with me.

"Nakdi, what were you thinking? You could have gotten yourself killed. You just can't go walk-in' into the house like that. You have to stay out here or in the fields if you wanna stay alive gal."

"Beta, what are you talk-in' bout. I didn't know I couldn't go in dare. Why you didn't tell me before now?"

"Fool child, don't you know these people own you. They can do whatever they want which you. They can kill you out in the open and ain't nobody gone do anything about it. We ain't free like we were back home to do what we want. Nakdi, things are different here. Life is different for us here."

~

My homeland, lush with green forage. Common reality for us was to run through the trees and just have fun as girls. My parents were ashamed of me and proud of me at the same time. They were ashamed of my physical attributes, but proud that I didn't let it stop me from being who I was. I protected the girls from the boys in our village who would try to be abusive. The trees were as tall as they wanted to be. Hearing the air ruffling through the leaves. We loved it even more when it rained. We would stand there and let the rain drops fall on our faces from the leaves twenty or more feet above.

As a child, I was mischievous and full of my father's characteristics. I was trustworthy and honest to a fault and didn't have a problem telling anyone what I thought about them, except for our Chief, the elders and my parents. My village was love and I loved my people, but they didn't know how to love me back. They didn't fight for us who were taken, and my parents didn't fight for me either. I was the oldest and they have my brother and sister to look after.

It was at that moment I looked at Beta and truly understood we were in a different place. I sat on the floor and wept, heartbroken, because I didn't belong there. Homesick, I was also ashamed of where I had come from.

~

Master Ben took an interest in me, why I didn't know. After a year, I was speaking and understanding their language and working in the field when Master Ben was away bringing more of us to this land that was not ours or theirs. It surprised most, but I didn't hesitate to talk to Beta in our native language every chance I got. I had learned more than most because I could.

Here, the Ghost's like Master Ben had taken this land from the Native people and they were doing the same to my people as well. I was angry as I learned the truth about it, but I could never be mad at Master Ben personally, because he grew up knowing no different either way, but that still was no excuse for it. It wasn't just rationale for what happened, but it was the reality of my existence. Think about it, if God is in control, then this too had purpose and meaning. Not that it was right or just, but purposeful.

Within two years, I was reading and working inside the house. I was glad to be out of the burning sun and Master Ben's personal servant. His mother only had use for me when she could not reach something, it was annoying to say the least. He felt free when I was around and didn't mind getting naked in front of me when he was gonna take a bath. Of course, I would have to make sure the water stayed a temperature he liked.

He would have me read to him while he was in the bath and even when he wasn't. He'd stand up in the bath and ask for a towel when he was finished. Most of the time, I think he did it to try and get a rise out of me or thought I would be shamed for what I saw and turn away, but I never did. I stood there with no reaction at all, because this was nothing new to me. He was just a ghost color. I think a part of me wanted to be his mother, because Mrs. Henderson never paid him any mind and neither did his father. At times, it seemed he was more of a captive than us. He had no choice who his parents were nor who he would marry.

They were up in age and eager for Master Ben to marry and have them some grandchildren. One day after one of his baths, he stood in front of me naked and told me he was getting married.

"Who is she Ben?" I wanted to seem interested, but I didn't care. He was now twenty-three and running his father's business and plantation.

"Her name is Susie and I've been courting her for five months now. I do not love her, but I recon I ain't getting any younger. I guess one day I will learn to love her like I'm supposed too, but for now we are trying to get to know each other."

He married Susie Stevens three months later and I had become her attendant too. She was shocked I could read and write and more, and that Ben allowed it. I would read to Ben before he'd go to sleep like he was a five-year-old child. I was a quiet soul, but I would tell the truth to anyone who would listen. Most of the time, it was to Beta.

One summer, "Wait a minute, Nana. I have to take a bathroom break."

"All right baby, you let me know when you are ready again."

"Okay."

I ran to the bathroom as fast as I could. When I got back to Nana's sitting room, she had taken a little nap and I didn't want to wake her. All I could think about at that moment was how precious this time meant to me and would I truly understand her story. All she went through as a slave. I hoped she wouldn't hold anything back from me. I guess if I think about it, she didn't have to tell me her life story at all.

Horror stories I had read in literature and was learning in my history class, was something I probably wouldn't be able to live through. Realizing that right now in 1940, the legalization of slavery was less than an eighty years ago, and we were still truly not free. I was thinking so hard that I think I woke Nana up from her nap and she brought me back to reality.

"I didn't know I had dozed off."

"Don't worry Nana, I want you to get as much rest as you need. Whenever you want to stop for the day, just let me know."

"Okay precious. I think I can go a little while longer. Where did I leave off?"

"You said you were going to talk about something that happened one summer."

"Yes, that's right."

One summer, Beta got sick. That summer, I was run ragged. I took care of the Henderson's during the day and Beta at night. Bacchus and Ancita helped with Beta during the day and I would sneak off during the day to check on Beta to make sure she had everything she needed while I was tending to the ghosts.' I thought I was going to lose my mind during that summer, because I owed Beta everything and I didn't want her to die and leave me alone there. Her fever would get so high, she was delirious sometimes. After two weeks, she finally got better and fully recovered after a month. Thank our Creator she didn't die, and they never caught me going back and forth.

# 3

## The Weaving Basket

Six months later, as I sat in the house library reading. Ben ran in and announced Ms. Susie's pregnancy with their first baby. Of course, I wasn't happy tending to her every demand, but now there would be another little life I could talk to and take care of that I liked more. Ben was home when the baby arrived and they named him Benjamin Jr. I had witnessed many babies delivered in my twenty-one-year life span, but no one screamed like Mrs. Susie. She shrieked and howled, and I was positive she would perish during childbirth. We couldn't help but laugh inside because this was part of our payback through God. Sure enough, she got through it, and the household calmed down and got back to routine. The family was overjoyed at his birth. There were smiles all around from the ghost folk. There was nothing in it for us but more labor.

A week later, Mrs. Susie gets up from the bed and she hadn't fed Jr. all night. When she goes to his bassinet, she discovers him not moving. A curdling scream startled everyone. We wanted her to suffer, but we didn't wish this. Nobody wanted to touch him to see if he was alive. Nobody took him except me. I was the only soul to hold his lifeless body. "Ben, call the doctor just to make certain, but he's not breathing," I said. There was no mistaking what this was. I put a mirror up to his nose and there was nothing. The doctor got there and pronounced little Benjamin dead. I was the only one who prayed over his soul. I wrapped his week-old body to be buried. They didn't want to bother with a funeral box nor have a gathering, so we, meaning me and Beta and some others, buried him at the family cemetery at the back of the plantation. It seemed to me cold and downright disgraceful. After burying little Benjamin, I went to Ben and asked him to get a gravestone for the baby and if he didn't, "You're being selfish and irresponsible." He turned around and slapped me. "You listen, and you listen good. You need to stay in your place, you hear me, Nakdi? Do I make myself clear?" I did not cry, but I said, 'Yes, sir,' with disdain. It took two to three years, but the day came I was dreading. I understood I was a slave and nothing more. From that point forward, I had to do the *Slavery Dance*. I hated him and our relationship as it was—was over. I realized I was living a fantasy and didn't have to experience what the others had to as a slave. Seeing the beatings, the hangings, and the torture, but because I hadn't experienced it myself, I thought I was different. A part of me could understand his anguish and sadness, because of the loss of his child, but never would I have thought he would hit me. I did the dance as their server. I didn't deviate one bit, and I didn't speak to him for months.

Times were getting tougher economically. Lynching's, killings, poor crops, and we were hearing about other slaves running away and going up north. We knew trouble was brewing everywhere. We just didn't know how bad it was going to get.

Three years later, civil war was upon us. Now twenty-five with no children of my own. Master Ben's parents had died a year apart from each other from complication of pneumonia. So, when he insisted on fighting in the war, he put Ms. Susie in charge. She was a blonde-haired, brown-eyed ghost that gave us all hell. She was not a gorgeous woman, but she was not plain either.

When Master Ben left the first time, Ms. Susie found out she was pregnant again and was as mean as anybody could be during her course of expectancy.

"Nakdi, come here. You come here quick gal!"

"Yes, Miss."

"You pick some fresh greens and get to cooking for my supper."

"Yes, Miss." She hauled off and slapped me for no reason. There was no reason other than to be evil.

This time, Master Ben knew nothing about the baby and by the time he got back after a year, the baby had been born and had expired a week later, just like Jr. No one ever reported to him about the second baby and Mrs. Susie, was in profound depression, so she wasn't revealing much of anything. Master Ben felt helpless because he was suffering a battle at home and on the battleground. He paid for the best doctors available, but nothing seemed to work for Mrs. Susie. Feeling hopelessness ever so creeping through his veins deeper. He fled back to the war.

Ten months after Master Ben being gone again, Beta ran down the stairs to get me, because Ms. Susie had laid up in the bed for over five months. Never getting up while none of us was present. Only accepting her tray of food as we left it at the door. I dashed up the stairs scared, perspiration rolling down my face, and all I heard coming from that room was screaming. I ran through the wood and Ms. Susie was in the bed panting and she continued to scream at the top of her lungs, because of the pain. At eleven at night, she was about to wake the dead. I drew back the sheets to check to see what was wrong and the baby's head had crowned. "Put a rag in her mouth, Beta, so she can bite down on it. Then go get some more cloths. This baby is coming right now." Beta runs to get water and more towels and by the time she gets back the baby was out and lying on the bed with the cord needing to be cut. Beta was an expert at delivering babies and she did what was necessary for a baby to live and for no infection to set up on Ms. Susie. We cleaned up the baby boy. We knew what Mrs. Susie had been up to when she would lock her door. Several times, when Beta or I would go to check on her to make sure she got up and not wallow in the bed all day from the depression, she'd lock her door. Calling out to her, she'd tell us to go away. We couldn't figure out how he got into her room with nobody seeing?

We kept the baby with Mrs. Susie to nurse, and it seemed like that was the only time she was in her right mind. Downstairs, we went into a room where no one could hear us talk.

"That baby ain't no full white baby, Nakdi."

"I know that Beta. I can see for myself." Pacing the floor for twenty minutes.

~

It shocked me to the core. I had known only what I read in our history. My mother never told me of the horrid things the masters did to the slave girls. So, I had to ask.

"Wait! Nana, you mean to tell me that baby was part colored?"

"Colored, I don't want you to use that word anymore, baby. We are Africans living in a country we have no business being in, but we're here. Your heritage is from Africa. I'd rather you use black because black is beautiful."

And just like that, my Nana went on with the story.

"Yes, and trust me, child. Just like you are shocked hearing it, we were just as shocked looking at him in the flesh."

~

I told Beta we couldn't allow anybody else to find out about the baby. "If any of Mr. Ben's men find out, they are going to kill every one of them men out there, just for being with a ghost woman and they may just kill Mrs. Susie too if she tells them she liked it."

I was trying to make light of the situation, but I also knew this was too dangerous to ignore. Not only did we have to worry about the ghosts on the plantation, but those that might visit. Her friends, although most never came when both her babies died. But her family lived not too far from here either. What if one of them comes to check on her?

"Nakdi, we have to get her to let us take the baby and let us raise him, if he lives more than a week. I'm telling you, there's a curse on Master Ben and Mrs. Susie with havin' babies. If this baby lives, she can't keep him."

"You know she's touched in the head right now."

"I wanna know who the pappy is, so we can beat him half to death ourselves. What was he thinkin'?"

"I know what he was thinking revenge. What's the best form of vengeance on another man? Get to his woman and that's just what he did, but I don't expect he was counting on this."

"I don't know who it is, but whoever it is, he touched too. Crazy in the head for being with a ghost woman period."

~

We allowed Ms. Susie to nurse the baby, but we also knew Master Ben would arrive home soon, unless he was lost in the war. Most of the time, she would lay catatonic and let him suckle, and other times, she would want to cuddle him. She was in and out of herself, but most, she was out. We had to watch her and would just stare at the sight of what used to be a whole woman. Beta and I felt bad for her more than anything. We could have taken our revenge on Ms. Susie if we wanted, because of how she treated us, but it would create more questions.

She was a trickery woman. One day, she had gone around the plantation whipping on whoever she could get a hold of. She didn't do it herself, but she had the ghost farmhands do it as she went around pointing at those, she wanted beaten. She had the lot hurting and they couldn't work for two days. Master Ben got so furious at her he was about to hit her but stopped short. I guess that was the first time we saw she was a little disturbed in the head. When he rebuked her for what she had done, she just got quiet and sat in her chair for two days, doing nothing at all. She'd slap Beta for no reason. It was like entertainment for her in that moment. I think she caused us pain to soothe her own grief. She could never reach me to slap me, but she would work me hard just to get even, just because she could. I think too, because Ben allowed me to read, she didn't much know how to read, she was jealous of what he had done for me.

We stood there staring at her one day. Wondering and scratching our heads at the events we were dealing with.

"Nakdi, I don't wish too much bad for Master Ben, but I'm hoping he doesn't come home. If he ever finds out about this baby and that it lived for over a month now, there's only two things gon' happen. One, he gonna kill her and then kill himself."

"Beta quit talking nonsense. We must get this baby off the land and into town, so someone else can find him and take care of him. The only way we're going to get this baby off the plantation, is when I run into town for supplies. We gonna have to take him and leave him someplace nobody can see us do it."

Ms. Susie was well enough to get out the bed and be free around the house, but it seemed like she was forever outside herself and had lost all memory of her just having a baby a month ago. Master Ben left Mr. Willie in charge after the second and third time he went off to fight in the war. Mr. Willie trusted me only to go into town by myself. That day came. We were out of supplies, not only for the farm, but for the house, too.

"Hey gal, I need you to go into town," Mr. Willie said.

"Mr. Willie, is it all right if I take Beta into town with me this time? I only ask Mr. Willie because we must bring back a lot of supplies. Everything is low, and it's gonna be a large order."

Mr. Willie hadn't said too much to me before, but he slammed me up against the side of the house and put his hands on my breast and touched me where no one had before. It horrified me since Master Ben wasn't there that Mr. Willie would seize the opportunity.

"What you gonna give me if I let Beta go, which you?" He said, as the vile stench came from his tobacco breath.

"Mr. Willie, I need Beta's help and you know Master Ben doesn't want nobody to touch me that way and if he finds out I ain't no virgin, I'm gonna have to tell him why I'm not anymore." He held me there for a few moments to think about what I had said, and he let me go, but before he did, he slapped me hard. Blood rand down my nose and mouth.

"You take Beta, which you and you better do as you always do and get back here gal."

"Yes, sir, Mr. Willie. You can trust us to do right. Plus, we don't want to leave Mrs. Susie too long." I clinched my body as tight as I could waiting for the next hit. He looked at me as though he had won and shouted loud enough for everyone to hear. "Go on and take Beta. I don't trust nobody else to take care of Mrs. Susie while ya'll go."

And as loud, "Yes, sir, Mr. Willie. It'll be quicker with Beta's help."

He walked towards the field and I ran from around the house with my arms flailing as fast as they would go to get away from Mr. Willie. I grabbed Beta's hand to get the baby in the basket.

"Beta, we gotta do it now."

"Nakdi, what do we have to do now?"

"Mr. Willie told me to take you to town with me to get supplies. When we go into town, we can take the weaving basket."

"Oh! The weave'n basket!" Beta said.

The look on Beta's face was heartbreak and fear. Beta had aged beyond her years, for fear consumed her often. I couldn't help but understand, but fear was something I could never allow to infiltrate my well-being. Yes, I had been scared many times and being around Mr. Willie was always scary, but I didn't fear him. I knew they could do with me whatever they wanted, and I was sure one day I would die by their hands, but I wouldn't be willing to go down without a fight. We had to get the weaving basket off the plantation for the baby to survive. We walked by Mr. Willie as though God designed and approved it himself. Maybe it was. All we could do was pray to the God who created us in the first place, that Mr. Willie wouldn't stop us to check to see what was in the weaving basket. We got on the wagon and didn't even look his way, and he didn't stop us. The baby never made a sound as though he knew we were trying to save his life from Master Ben and premature death. We covered him under ivory colored yarn and set out for town, and from time to time we would check on him as we went. Beta drove the wagon and when it was clear, I took the baby out and held him in my arms as if he was mine. I had no child of my own and by this time. I didn't think I ever would. Master Ben made it clear to every man on that plantation and any other plantation that I was off limits. Before he had the notion to get married or go off to war, he had gathered all the men on the plantation, ghost and African alike. "It is a rarity that I make such a request or demand on my staff about a niggra gal. I recon, it will be an experiment of mine, but I want it followed without question." He grabbed me by the hand and put his fingers through mine. "Nakdi here is off limits to every white or negro man on or off this plantation. I will choose the man I want to mate with her. Do I make myself clear?" He looked around at them all and then stopped at me. I didn't know the language then, but Beta told me later what he had said. "If I catch any man looking her way in a lustful manner, I will kill you on the spot and I mean that for the white and the niggra men too." From that day, no one would ever look my way, unless I just said hello to them, but I wouldn't say anything to the ghosts at all. I was damaged goods without even being touched. My life was dealing with the Misses, the house, and the children that would roam around while the parents would work in the fields.

Riding in the wagon with Ms. Susie's and the mystery man's baby, I thought to lie and say I found him abandoned on the road and take him for myself since I was lonely and wanted to be loved by anybody, but I couldn't take the chance Ms. Susie would recognize him and disclose information or the father would come forward and get his fool-self killed. We had no choice but to keep to our original plan. I think I prayed hard somebody would find the baby fast, because we couldn't be too late in getting back. Mr. Willie would come looking for us.

When we arrived in town, everyone recognized us—especially me. After a few hellos, they paid us no mind in what we had to do to get the supplies and get back. I left the baby at the back of the doctor's office and sure enough, a woman came out and almost tripped over the weaving basket, as she was talking to some other ghost lady and wasn't paying attention to where she was walking. She looked to be a ghost, but when I saw she was carrying the bags of her ghost misses, I thought all hope was lost. When she picked up the basket to move it to the side and right on cue, the weaving basket cried. She looked inside and, of course, Beta was getting the supplies while I was trying to watch and see who would take the weaving basket for sure. I could see everything, as she moved the yarn from the side. She threw the yarn to the ground and took Lil' Mister out of the basket. They were talking low, so I couldn't hear what they were saying. Finally, the miss took Lil' weave'n basket from the almost ghost African lady and took him into the doctor to be checked, I could only hope. Creeping, but walking up to the doctor's window to see them loving on him already. The misses were talking and kissing on the baby like he was her own.

~

Nakdi turned her attention to her great-granddaughter. "You know Nakida, I didn't care who took the baby and loved it. Just knowing he would live. I didn't want to let him go and when I saw he was going to go home with someone else, I cried like a baby. I ran toward where Beta was getting the supplies and I couldn't stop crying."

~

When we got back on the road, I continued to cry for the boy. Beta cried and got mad at me for crying and making her cry.

"Nakdi, stop crying. We did what we had to do for him to survive in this cruel and punishing existence. If he can have a better life than what we had, then we done our duty to God and that boy." It was as if the roles had reversed. Beta the wreck was making sense of the situation. I think it was the relief she had of not hiding the boy anymore.

"I know Beta, but we may never know what happens to the boy."

"Nakdi, the boy is in God's hands now. All we can do is wish for the best life he could get and hope it's better than what we got."

"I have no life, Beta. I've never had a child growing inside of me. Master Ben's hex cursed me to be barren for life. Never to love or be loved by another man. I'm twenty-six and not one man has ever looked at me like they look at you, Beta. You've had children Beta. You know what it's like to have a brand-new person growing inside of you."

"Yes Nakdi, but you've never had to experience having that child ripped from your arms and taken somewhere else as payment for a debt. You never had a child torn from your arms to be killed by the hand of your Misses because they don't want another mouth to feed or she knows it's her husband's child and she doesn't want it to live. You never had one of your children killed, because you made your Misses angry cause you spilled soup on her new dress at a dinner party. Nakdi, you never had a child come out dead, because massa beat you so, because you fought back from him gettin' on top of you while you far long into the pregnancy."

Seeing the tears just fall as we continued back to the house. I closed my mouth and didn't say another word about my life or the lack thereof. I had nothing to groan about anymore. I had nothing but my existence.

# 4

## The War Comes Home

As we approached the plantation, we saw everybody standing around and even Mr. Willie. As we rode up, I saw him looking like hell itself was standing there. I was the only one who jumped off the wagon and ran to him. He stood there beaten and worn to his very core. He stood there trembling like a schoolboy, clothes torn and black ash and dirt smeared everywhere. He smelled like death had passed through and around his body. He was terrified and looked at me in my face as he had done so many times before and said, "The war is over," while crying and breaking down in front of everyone. "The other side won." He looked at me and said, "You are free to go." He started screaming and hollering that everyone was free to get off his land if they wanted to. Mr. Willie ran over to him to stop him from saying what he had said and hit Master Ben until he was unconscious.

Most of us didn't move because we didn't know what he meant about us being free. I had asked some of the men to help me get Master Ben up to his room. Most of the men walked away back to their shacks and only two of the men left standing there helped me get him in the house. I saw that look of fear on Beta's face again. It was almost like she went into instant panic mode. The old Beta was back. That fierce woman on the buggy was no more.

The men grabbed Master Ben and I grabbed Beta and almost slapped her, but I shook her instead, to keep it together. I got Ben undressed as much as I could and left him in the bed to sleep and he slept and slept.

Later that night, the moon was full and the silence was deafening. I didn't know what to think or what to say to anyone. It was an eerie feeling as though you knew something was going to happen, but you had no clue as to what. Late in the midnight hour when most was sleep, some of the African men got a hold of Mr. Willie and killed him dead. It was as quiet as a church mouse around there for the next few days and no one came looking or asking about Mr. Willie and they never found his body. What they had done to him, we never knew. There was a quiet uprising on the Henderson Plantation. Some of the men left that night Mr. Willie went missing for the pure joy that they were free men per Mr. Benjamin Henderson. Others left because of fear that Mr. Willie was nowhere to be found and they didn't want to be blamed for it or for just knowing what happened that night. I had heard that some of the escaped men made it to Chicago and others weren't that lucky and died in their temporary freedom being caught by other plantation ghost workers for running away.

There were no riots on the plantation, no one decided to burn down the house or the barn and everything stayed quiet for the next three nights. Even though he had said we were free, we really weren't. There was nowhere for most of us to go. I watched over Ben for those three days, while Beta watched over Mrs. Susie. When he finally woke up, he was still a little groggy and I had asked Beta to ride into town to get Doctor Porter. I stayed by his side until the doctor came in all panicky and acting like Beta. I'm sure she had something to do with his anxiety. She was good for telling other harm may come to you. "What's wrong with him gal and why didn't you call me earlier?" Doctor Porter was very indignant, that's just how it was. Some of them ghosts were humbled at the fact they could no longer hold us against our will and others were so downright mean and vicious, we had to pick and choose who to fight back with. Dr. Porter was one of those I wasn't getting ready to take no mess from. "Dr. Porter, the reason I didn't call you earlier, I was concerned for your safety. I mean, coming out here a few days ago, may have been a death sentence for a man such as yourself coming way out here, just like you are now." He looked at me with such fear. It scared me to know I had such power now, but I didn't want any other ghosts coming out trying to establish the kind of order I was used to seeing. I walked to the other side of the bed where he was standing and looked him in his eyes—kind of standing over him. "Dr. Porter, I need you to check him thoroughly and make sure he will get better. He's been sleeping for three days. I check his breathing often. I know what this war has done to him, and I need to make sure you get him better." He knew I meant business, he also realized I wanted Ben to get better, and I meant him no harm. I could have run off like some of the others who were trying to find their family members that had been sold off, but to where was I going to go? I had no family to find. All I knew was Ben had never done me any harm physically, except that one time and he wasn't like some of the other Master Ghost's I had heard about on other plantations.

~

"Nana, didn't you want to leave just for the fact that they took you from your home?"

"Child, of course, I could have run off and been free to roam to wherever I could get too or die by some other ghosts, but to where was I going to run? Those others nor I had freedom papers. Ben had to get better for that to happen. I knew nobody but Beta and others on that plantation. Beta was my best friend. No man could approach me for marriage, so there was no other man I could run off with. I guess I could have just left for the principle of the whole thing, but I also didn't want to leave without Beta and she wasn't going anywhere. She was too afraid to leave. I had no clue how to get back to my family in Africa and everyone on the Henderson Plantation was my family now. Even though I had never been beaten into submission like the others physically, I had been beaten mentally into believing there was nothing else out there for me. Even if I had left, what was I going to do for money? I had been taken care of for nine years."

"I understand Nana, if you want to quit for the day, that's fine. We can continue tomorrow."

"Don't worry about me baby. I'll let you know when I'm tired."

"Okay, Nana."

~

After the doctor looked Ben over and diagnosed him with plain exhaustion, if he did wake up, what was he going to be like? He had fought hard for the Confederacy. We had no clue as to whom and what would wake up. Would he accept the defeat and treat us like human beings or would he hold hatred in his heart for us? Even before the civil war started, we could so rarely meet some ghostly men and women who would be against slavery that was going on in the South and just as fast as they would ride into town to say their peace, they would be run out of town just as quickly.

Mr. Willie was gone, the rest of the men that stayed on continued to take care of the crops and farm animals as Beta had asked them too. I pretty much stayed by Ben's side and nursed him back to health. He would toss and turn and scream out at night and then would fall back into unconscious sleep.

Two days after Dr. Porter checked him over, he finally woke up to see me sitting on the bed next to him.

"How long have I been back and how long have I been out?"

"You have been back for five days and you been asleep for those five days too."

"Has Susie come in to check on me?"

I didn't want to tell him Mrs. Susie was completely lost in the mind, right away, because I didn't know how he would take it, but this was something you don't keep quiet.

"Mrs. Susie has not been well since you been gone to war the last time. She sick in the head and I don't think she's ever coming back to you. You been gone for over a year and because we are not her family, you the only one who can put her somewhere and she might get better. She don't talk at all and all she does is lay in her bed or stare out the window when I make her get up out the bed. I went to get her folks to come out to see her, but they refused."

"Yeah, they had a difference of opinion about our marriage and how Susie didn't need them anymore. They pretty much disowned her, except they wanted to see their grandchildren."

"Right now, I'm going to get you something to eat to build your strength and when you are able, we have a lot to talk about."

For the first time, Ben looked at me with such regret and there was misfortune in his eyes. He was lost and I could see it, but I was the one to bring him back to the reality of things. I had brought him up some broth and made him drink it and hoped he wouldn't get sick from not eating before.

The next morning, I brought him some toast and juice to drink and by the evening, he was out of bed and walking around his room. When I came in to check on him, he was sitting on the side of his bed sobbing. I walked back out and didn't bother him anymore that night.

At daybreak, everything was working like it had always been and now Daniel was in charge. He was the oldest on the farm and had been there longer than anybody else. He knew the plantation backward and forward and it was the only full functioning plantation for miles and the strangest thing, ghost men would come there to ask for work after returning from the war. It would get testy sometimes with ghosts coming to the plantation for work and an African turning them away, but they couldn't do anything when all the rest of the plantation workers would stand behind Daniel and the other ghosts would not come to their rescue and tell them there was no work there for them. It was a strange time, but we were grateful for that moment, because we certainly didn't know how long it was going to last.

I was up bright and early and as I was walking up the stairs to bring Ben and Mrs. Susie some breakfast, I saw Ben walking into Mrs. Susie's room. She was already up and sitting in the chair staring out the window. Unknowing, I walked in behind him. He called out her name and she gave no response. He walked over to her and stood there in front of her like that was going to make a difference in her reality. She looked up at him and smiled and turned away like he was a stranger passing by. I walked in and stood by her chair.

"Ben, I told you she is sick in the head. She doesn't know who you are anymore."

He knelt at her feet. "Susie, do you know who I am?" She gave no response and turned and continued to look outside the window. It wasn't until then I knew who the daddy was of that boy. Rudy was just as simple as she was mentally out of herself, but somehow, they had formed a connection with each other that continued.

"Ben, I need you to understand she's not coming back to you and she needs to be in that place with the doctor's."

"I know it's my fault she's like this, I shouldn't have left her."

"It wasn't you leaving that caused this. It was because she couldn't have them babies survive. If those babies were living, she would be as happy as rain on a hot summer day. After the last one died…"

"What do you mean last one? I thought it only happened once!" The pain on his face was if he had died on that battlefield. His hair was matted down to his head and so was his beard. To smell him, I knew he hadn't bathed in months. His hands and skin where dry and cracked as wood board gets wet and then dry up again. And I didn't know if his feet would ever heal from the soars. He would have sat there in grief if I hadn't made him get up and go back to his room. I had decided right then and there, I couldn't let them both go crazy, or all of us would be in trouble.

That night, I had run him a bath and sat him in it for as long as I needed to change his bed linen, cut his hair, and shave him. When I got him out of the tub, I cleaned and dressed every wound on his body the natural eye could see. I read to him every night like I had done before for three days straight.

On Saturday morning, two weeks after he had arrived from the war, I walked in the room, and he was already dressed.

"Nakdi, I need you to get Mrs. Susie ready to go to the psychiatry hospital. I sent a letter to Dr. Porter and he's going to meet us there. Can you pack her things, especially her favorite trinkets? I want her to be at peace and I'm not sure she can be that here."

"Okay, Master. Ben."

"Please stop calling me Master Ben. Ben or Benjamin will do just fine."

I guess I had reverted to my old ways since he was up and seemed to be doing better. I called him Ben the whole time I took care of him. He was sick like he was my child, and the burden was all mine.

"Nakdi, I want you to go with us. She knows you better than she knows me. She responds to you."

"Okay, I will let you know when she is ready."

He hadn't stepped foot outside the house for those two weeks. When I got Mrs. Susie ready to go, I brought her down the stairs. When we got down to the bottom of the stairs, the front entry way was wide open and all that was left of us was standing there looking at Ben sobbing on his knees. He sobbed so much. I didn't think he was ever going to stop. I walked out the door and proceeded to get on my knees to console him and he grabbed onto me and held me tight. He finally stopped after fifteen long minutes and then he got up and did something I had never seen him do before. He went to each one he had bought or taken from Africa and hugged them and told them he was sorry. Why? I don't know. I had my suspicions. Could it have been that things were changing, and he was truly no longer in charge? Could it have been that with the change that had come, he could lose everything? I was thinking it and I was certain the rest of us was thinking it. We was just grateful the old Master Ben didn't come back from the war.

I had never seen such a thing in my whole entire life. I even saw Mr. Daniel shed a tear. Ben's daddy had sold off his wife and children to pay a debt and Mr. Henderson had never said he was sorry for having to do it. I guess it overwhelmed him that the farm was still going and operational. We were grateful though, he never asked about Mr. Willie, and we didn't have to lie.

At this point, I didn't know whether he was doing this because we hadn't left him. After all the spectacle of apologies, he got up on the wagon and waited for me to bring Susie out to take her to the mental place. I told Beta where we were going and to keep an eye on the place until we got back.

~

Questioning my Nana again, "How much had things changed now the war was over where you were from?"

"Well, put it this way. There were still a lot of ghost men and women who hated our very existence. They didn't feel like we were anywhere close to being as superior as they thought they were. They didn't believe we were human beings. We were bread as animals. Not all the ghosts felt that way, but the majority down south felt that way and they tried their best to keep us in the existence of bondage, even though we were legally free to a certain extent. They didn't have to do much to keep us in line, most of us had known nothing else. We hadn't got educated like you all today. That's why I stress education to everyone. We should never be in that situation again.

They continued to kill us without cause or justification and it was only on the merit of our skin color and the misuse of the word of God. They had forgotten to read where God had brought the Israelites out of slavery and bondage, because they had been mistreated so. Sometimes I look at our people today and think, we have been free for a long time, but we act like we still slaves to our circumstances and we act like we are still in bondage. Anyway, baby, it's getting late and I'm finally tired. You come back tomorrow, and we'll continue."

"Alright Nana, you get some rest and I'll call you before I come."

"Okay, you be safe."

~

The next day, I got to the house as fast as my legs and the bus could take me for Nana to continue with her history. She was bright eyed, bushy tailed and raring to go. I sat down next to her on the couch and was raring to hear more. My life existed because of Nana and her life, which became my history as well.

"Let's see, where did I leave off?"

"You were on your way to take Mrs. Susie to the mental hospital."

"Awe, yes. That's right."

# 5

## The Special Pendant

The ride was long and bumpy. Our bodies swayed back and forth in silence for all those miles. When we reached the psychiatry place, Dr. Porter was waiting for us and, of course, he said nothing to me and I said nothing to him. Our understanding was unspoken in body language. We walked Ms. Susie in and they had a room waiting and her own personal dresser drawers. I set up all her little trinkets she loved and put her clothing in the drawers and walked out of the hospital. I didn't like that place, the wailing and women wandering around talking to themselves and the walls. The walls oozed sadness. Walking out, I relaxed in the wagon, so I could give them some private time alone. It was only about ten minutes before Ben came out. He gave Dr. Porter a handshake and walked to the wagon in silence again.

While sitting in the wagon on the way home, it was at that very moment, it felt like I was free to do whatever I wanted. I jumped out of the wagon and started running in the open field on the left and the right of us. Ben stopped and just looked at me as though he wanted to be free too, but conflict was ever present in that head of his. It was like that ten-year-old girl was running through the jungle of my village again. I had never forgotten about her or my home, what it was like to breathe there, how we loved, laughed, and took care of each other. For that moment, I was there with my friends, laughing and yelling loud.

Falling on the ground to catch my breath, Ben ran over to me to see if I was alright. When he reached me, I was laughing, and he held out his hand. I took it and that's when I saw a ghost man coming with a gun behind him. I told Ben the ghost man was coming and when he turned around, the man was pointing the long gun at Ben's head and asked him, "Are you a nigga lover? Why you lettin' this nigga gal run all over my field like you own it or something? Get this nigga gal off my property, before I kill her where she stands and you too, for allowing her to do it. What kind of nonsense is this going on here? Why you are letting her run free around here. Ain't nothing changed and it ain't gonna change as long as there is breath in my body."

Ben stood straight and broad shouldered and put his hands up to calm the ghost man down, if that was at all possible. I didn't know.

"Kind, Sir, I apologize for any inconvenience this has caused, but you don't have to come out with a gun. Nakdi here was just stretching her legs. We have traveled such a long way and we just on our way back."

"Since the war been over, there's been a lot of nigger uprising's out here. I didn't see you at first. Tell me what town you from?"

"Good, Sir, if you must know, we are on the outskirts of South Carolina. I own the Henderson Plantation there."

"You get her out of here now."

The whole time, I was hiding behind Ben, horizontal wise, I realized we weren't free at all. Ben grabbed my hand, and he led me to the wagon. I was about to get on the back, and he told me to sit next to him. I didn't realize until later why he made me sit with him. Ben figured if the man shot at me, he would shoot Ben as well, so he would more than likely not shoot at me if Ben was next to me. "We have to be careful not to upset the locals down here. No law right now will keep these folks from killing anything that moves with colored skin." I never once took my eyes off the ghost man until we were out of his sight. I think by that time, I was breathing again. I didn't say or do anything the rest of the ride back to Henderson, and neither did Ben.

~

On Sunday morning, we all woke up to a bell ringing. Ben was calling a meeting to talk to all of us. We all stood around waiting for him to talk in the already blistering sun. "I know that some of you were here when my daddy was alive, and he didn't treat most of you right. Making no excuse because I did the same for fear of my father. I am asking all of you to stay and work, so we all will survive, and I will pay you for your labor. I promise to never cheat you, but I also don't want to be taken advantage of, either. We will work together. You will get paid for the work you do around here, and that includes the women working in the house. Right now, I don't know how much I'm going to pay you, but it will be fair. We will meet again soon."

All the following week, Ben left the plantation to meet with the townspeople about seed and lumber. On Saturday, he came back angry and later than usual. They had accused him of saying he would pay the slave the same as he would the white folks. He had said what he said in front of everybody on the farm. We knew he wouldn't be able to do it and live, because someone would spread that information, just as it had.

Months later, he walks into the bedroom as I was changing his linen and about to get the bath water, he grabbed my hand and told me to get the bath ready and to bring a pitcher of goats mild and oatmeal. The way he looked at me scared me for a brief second. I ran to get what he asked for and brought it back up as fast as I could. There were rose pedals already in the water. He took the milk and the oatmeal and poured it in steaming water and told me to get in. I didn't know what to say or to do. He was just as tall as I was, so I knew I couldn't get away and live. He had locked the door to the bedroom and the windows was closed. There was nowhere I could run. I dropped my dress and got in, watching his every move. Once in, he turned towards the tub and knelt on the floor beside the tub and washed my body. "Nakdi, thank you for all these years of service and taking care of me and Ms. Susie like you did. I want you to know I was never like my father. I never wanted to treat any of you like he did. Once I was old enough, I could do things my way." He stopped the sponge at my breast. "I've loved you since the day we put you on the Majestic, but I could never show my feelings for you here until now. If my father was alive today, he'd hang me alongside you, just for thinking the way I do." He got up off his knees and went to the jewelry box that was on his dresser. He came back to the tub. "My grandmother gave me this before she died. I was to give this to my wife." He knelt again and dangled the necklace in my face. It was a silver pendant rose with a diamond in the middle. "I want you to have it as a gift of my love for you."

For the first time, I had no words, but unafraid of his love for me. For I had suppressed my feelings for him all these years. He put it around my neck. He walked away and looked outside the window that was reflecting the light from the lamp burner.

"You are not saying anything in return. I need to know if you feel the same about me."

"Hand me a towel, Ben. I stood up, unafraid for him to see my body. He walks over to the tub with the bath towel. I get out and stand in front of him. "I love you too, Ben. More than you will ever know." I kissed him, and he kissed me with vigor.

Breaking from his embrace, I couldn't help it, it was as if something was nudging me to be honest about what I felt. I told him, "I trusted you when you protected me on the boat. I loved you because you taught me your language and allowed me to read and write. You broke my heart when you slapped me for telling you the truth. I hated you because you allowed no one to touch me. I want to be married and have babies and be someone's, Benjamin. I will accept nothing less. I will not give you what you so desire without it being right before God. You could take me and there's not much I could do about it, but I would hate you and not love you as I do now"

"What is it you want me to do?" he asked.

"You will need to divorce Ms. Susie and marry me. I will not be your mistress or someone you can just lie with. I know there are those who want to keep me as their servants, but I am no longer a slave to anyone. I will not be a slave to you in this house. I want it to be proper and I don't care about what the other ghosts think. God's love is unconditional, but mine is not! I also want my free papers and for everyone else to get their Freedom papers."

"I will do your Freedom Papers and everyone else's tomorrow, but we won't get a minister to marry us down here. You have got to be reasonable about this. They would rather lynch both of us than to marry us."

"Take us up north for us to be married, before we can ever be together." I walked over to him and kissed him. "Benjamin, I want to have the children we deserve to have. I want us to share our love and be together, so we are going to do this the right way." I put back on my dress and walked out of his bedroom.

~

"Wow. Nana, you held out for love, and you were taking a risk in talking to him like that. Did he ever divorce Ms. Susie?"

"Because of her mental instability, it wasn't long before he got the divorce from Ms. Susie. Back then, all he had to do was file papers of divorce. She couldn't contest it, so it went through easy. After all that was happening between Ben and me, I had to tell someone, and I sat down with Beta and told her everything, because she was my best friend."

~

He had given everyone their Freedom Papers, and some did leave, but most were like me. They had no family to find, and they didn't have anywhere else to go, so they stayed and worked. I now had the freedom to go about the plantation as I pleased, and I took Beta down to the brook to talk.

"Ben and I are in love and we're going up north to get married."

"Why didn't I know before now? I'm supposed to be your friend."

"Beta, it's a dangerous time right now. We can't just go around talking about it to everyone. They didn't win the war, and their minds haven't changed about us being slaves. We want to get married and when things calm down around here, then we'll be able to share our love with the world."

"Nakdi, don't be fooled by this war being over or because Master Ben done apologize, that some of them men out there don't still hold anger in their hearts. Nakdi, if you go out there letting them men know you and Master Ben together, don't think they not goin' to be upset about it. They gonna say Master Ben planned this all along, that's why he forbid everybody else from asking for your hand. Nakdi, Master Ben's father, didn't ask for our hand or treated us like we were human beings. He took us whenever he wanted. Whether it was me or my daughter, his own daughter, Nakdi. He was a sick man. What makes you think Master Ben is so different?"

Tears rolled down and all I could do was wipe them away. I didn't know what to say. I loved Ben just as much as he loved me. There was that nagging tingle on the back of my neck because I couldn't know that he would follow through until he either did or didn't.

~

"Nana, didn't you realize what that meant back then? For you, a slave to marry a man that took you captive. Took you from your family. He forbids them from looking at you or even marrying you. It was like the white man had won again."

"Nakida, you don't think I understood what I was doing. The hatred still surrounding us like a ring of fire. Don't you think I cared enough about my people? Of course, I did. I love everything about us and who they are and what they were and what they had to endure, but love is not about what other people feel about another person's background and culture and what they've gone through. Was I to be with another African man just because of our skin color. The love of my people had nothing to do with me falling in love with Ben. I didn't love him out of knowing nothing else. I could have said to Ben, I didn't love him, and he needed to allow me to fall for someone else, but I didn't, because I knew I had the freedom in that aspect of life. At that moment, I had a choice—my choice. The only choice I could grasp as my own. I made the choice for where we were because I sure wouldn't be able to do it outside of there. I fell for him, as you young people say these days. Was I to deny what I felt, despite what others thought about me? It was dangerous either way, but love outweighed that danger. I had no obligation to anyone."

"Nana, what if he had treated you the way the other white people had, do you think you would have fallen in love with him?"

"No. I couldn't be with a man that could be cruel. I saw Ben when he was around every day and not once did, he ask or do the deed of beating us or lynching us. It was his daddy and Mr. Willie. He never requested it and when he could, he didn't allow it to happen, but this was not just a test for me. He was putting his life on the line as well. I was not the only one taking the risk. I make no excuse for what they did to us, but I make no excuse for my love, either. That's why I knew what had to be done."

"Nana, great grandpa benefitted from slavery."

"Yes, he and his family did. Unfortunately, so have I, but I'll tell you about that later in the story. Don't forget, our people aren't the deceivers, but we sure have some of the blame of how we got here."

~

It took a month before he could get the dissolution papers and that next week, we were heading up north to be married. We took Beta to be a witness to our union. Leaving with my people and his unaware of our plans, and Mr. Jameson was left in charge of the farm. We headed off to Chicago, Illinois, where we heard kept slaves were running too. It was 1863, taking us a week and a half to get there. Beta and I hid in the wagon until we were out of the southern states. We would park at night and sleep in the wagon, so we didn't have to be seen by nobody and Ben didn't have to answer questions about us, but he had our papers of freedom with him, just in case. We would lie on the ground and just look at the stars and wonder what Chicago would be like. I had only been in two places my whole existence—Africa and here. We would often think about the farm and wondered if everything was alright. The ghost men were evil and if they had any thought of what Ben and I were getting ready to do, they would have burnt the place down to the ground and killed everything that moved thereafter. To be free, we didn't know or realize the concept. To be in love with a ghost man was unconscionable to some, but was it uncommon? Yes, I had to say, but it happened on some plantations. The only difference was their ghosts weren't marrying the African women they loved. Was that love at all or convenience for the ghost man?

When we entered the bustling town, it was like no place I had ever seen or even heard of. The obvious was I had been in no other place, but it was shocking and for Beta, she could not have imagined the spectacle of sights. Beta was scared out of her wits, and there was a spark of excitement that lit her every being. The women like us were wearing big, long, fancy laced dresses. It was almost angelic to think we could wear such garments. To see how we had escaped the master's hand, mine through love and theirs through war and running.

We were there for two days. I could see we weren't property and bound anymore, but we weren't free. There were laws still holding us hostage, and the minds of some held us hostage as well. We had tried to find a justice of the peace to marry us, but none of the ghosts would. They would marry two ghosts and two Africans, but a White man and an African woman marrying, it was an anomaly and utter outrage to most of the ghost preachers. We went back to our room we rented in a black part of town. Beta had somehow come out of her shell and walked around Chicago as if she knew what she was doing and where she was going.

The third night, Beta came to me and told me there was an African preacher that would marry us, for a price, of course. I had told Ben about it and he agreed to pay. It wasn't as official as I would have liked, but it was before God, that's all that mattered to me at this point. We left the room and followed Beta to the preacher man and he married us for ten dollars. The preacher submitted the record to the registry without us, so it wouldn't get rejected and be unofficial. Ben's family had money, but he knew being with me, money meant little when it went against the grain of the confederacy and their backward thinking. Returning to the room, Ben offered Beta compensation to pay for a room of her own.

~

"Wait Nana, you don't have to get too descriptive here! It was your wedding night. I get it."

"Nakida, I am not ashamed of my love for your great-grandfather. We made love for the first time and as much as I wanted him, and he wanted me. It hurt like the dickens, but he was gentle and loving through the process. He had once again asked Beta to take care of me and two days later we could enjoy each other as husband and wife should."

~

We left Chicago after a week's time and headed back to South Carolina. We dreaded the ride home, but happy to be going home to see those we had left behind. After arriving home and seeing the farm still running well, we could rest for a few days without too much interruption. I would still get up and cook breakfast for Ben, but now it was out of love and not servitude.

We had been back for a month when I reached the bedroom and opened the door. The tray dropped to the floor and me to my knees. Ben ran over to me and helped me up and carried me to our bed.

"Honey!" Ben ran as fast as I've ever seen him, and he was holding Beta's hand when they ran in.

Beta sat next to me on the bed. "Nakdi, what happened?"

"I was lightheaded, and the room started whirling." She pulled my dress up and touched my stomach and began pressing hard.

"Nakdi, what do you feel when I press here?"

"I feel pressure and its tender but there's no actual pain."

"Well, it looks like you are going to have a baby."

Ben was excited, but he also saw fear in mine. "Beta let me talk to Nakdi please."

"Ben, I didn't want this to happen right away, but it has, and we can't raise our babies here. We just can't stay here with the way things are. I hate to say this, but if nothing had changed during the war, we could get away with it, but now everybody will know we've been together, and we won't be able to hide our love or this baby. I don't know what we're going to do, but we have to leave here before this baby comes or they will kill both of us."

He got up and lay next to me. He put his hand on my stomach and then kissed it. "Our child is growing in there, and I will make sure I protect both of you. I just need some time to figure out what I need to do."

"Well, you've got about eight months to figure it out. After I show, I won't be able to go out. I mean, people outside of this farm will not know or care I'm pregnant, but those on this farm are going to ask questions. Everybody is not loyal to you, Ben, African or white. Most of the men on this farm are here because they need to work, and they need to feed their families. Your kin folk won't like the fact you married an African woman, and those men out there just as well turn you over to the lynch mob to save their own skin. Ben, I love you because you are not like the people who hate us. Even though you fought in a war to keep us slaves, I know you had to do what you felt like you needed to do to survive. I don't want to be without you, but this child is most important to me, and I'd rather leave everything behind than try to hold on to it and lose us and this baby."

To leave it all behind was the most troubling of everything. He had sold his father's tobacco business in town within a month, but no one was buying land for what it was worth. He had a couple of offers, but they weren't worth selling to. Ben invited one of the potential buyers for dinner and, of course, we had to hide the fact I was his wife. I was three months pregnant by then and had a minor bump I could still hide under a large dress. It was an awful feeling to pretend to still be a slave in my home, but I had to realize it wasn't my home. It belonged to Ben's family. They housed there the captive and taken on that land. They built it on the backs of slaves, and I did not want to raise my children there. I would bring food out to the dining area and once I had brought everything out for supper with Beta's help.

I was about to sit down at the table. "Gal, what are you doin'?" Mrs. Dunham said. "Don't you know your place?"

She hadn't even noticed my dress was not like a slave or that I stood next to Ben when they arrived. When we were in Chicago, Ben bought me a few of the dresses we saw the other African women wearing.

Ben snapped, and even I couldn't hold Ben back. "Mr. and Mrs. Dunham, I am afraid I must ask you to leave our home and this property and never come back. This is no longer a slave plantation where these men and women must do what we tell them to do. Nakdi is a free woman, and I asked her to sit here to have a conversation with you Mrs. Dunham while I talk business with your husband and you all can talk lady talk, but you have come into my home and insulted us and now, I feel you are undeserving of our house or our farm. So now, I bid you all ado, goodbye."

Oh, yes, there was steam coming out of their ears and I don't think it was so much that Ben was kicking them out, but as they were getting on their coach to leave, Ben told them I was smarter and were more intelligent than they were, and they were stupid. I was proud of Ben, but I also knew I was right about leaving this place and never looking back. Ben then let his cousin Odell and his family run the farm and live there for free, but it would be only under the condition those who stayed on could continue working and living on the plantation for a fair wage.

~

"Nakida, I didn't know at the time Ben was worth millions even back then, but you wouldn't have known it."

"Well, Nana, great grandpa had sold the tobacco shop in town, he still had the farm."

"Come to find out, he had other houses in Mississippi that his father owned. Other plantations managers ran them."

"Where did you and great grandpa end up?"

~

The day we were leaving the Henderson Farm, I was eight and a half months. We thought we could get where we were going in about a week's time and have the baby in our new home, but before we could leave, I had contractions. Beta was there to help me and I had George that day. We had to stay on the farm, which meant we couldn't leave for another four months, due to winter. During the winter months, Ben continued to work and help on the farm while he doted on me and baby George.

Beta came in one day and I told her to sit next to me. "I know you're worried about Ben and me, but we are going to be fine and so are you. If something were to happen to us, I want you to raise George and any other children we may have. No matter where we are, I want you to be their second mother." Beta started crying as if I was dying. All I could see to do was to console her and understand.

"We're going down to Louisiana to the Vieux Carre' and we want you with us. I can't leave you here."

"Oh Nakdi! I love you so much. What am I going to do in Louisiana?" She started crying again.

"You can do whatever you want. You are free to live anywhere now. You can live with us or you can work for somebody else, and live in your own place, but I can't leave my sister here. I am ashamed I didn't think about it before now. You never know, you might find you a husband down there."

"Oh hush! I too old to be tryin' to find a husband."

"Beta, what are you talking about? You are only thirty-five and you are smart and beautiful on the outside and on the inside. Any man would be lucky to marry you. We are going to find somebody to take care of the baby for a few hours and we gonna go to school and do some more learning. Wherever they accept us for schooling, we gonna go together. After, you can work in a doctor's office. You know more about medicines than most doctors."

# 6

# The Vieux Carre' & Black Codes

## The Vieux Carre'

The ferocious winter we had to endure was finally over, and we headed to Louisiana at the first sign of spring. Ten days of travel was enough to drive anybody mad, but we had faired more than most. To leave South Carolina's devastation and head through greater devastation was more than we could comprehend. Passing by plantations burned to the ground and death all around—Africans and Whites alike. At first seeing this, suggested we made a mistake and would fare better back in Carolina. Dead and rotting bodies on the side of the road. It brought back memories of *Us* on the ships. Children sitting in squalor and wailing in the distance. I wanted to help the children, but Ben asked me not to. "Nakdi, we don't know if they have any diseases. We can't risk George getting sick." My heart broke, and it went out to them, but I could do nothing. It didn't matter to me whether they were ghost or African. I cried the final two miles until we reached Vieux Carre'.

New Orleans had fared better than most other Southern States. They surrendered early in the war and the Union Army took over the city. When we arrived, it was a bustling town, but not a city like Chicago. There were plenty of folk looking for work and kids playing in the streets. Those long petticoat dresses made it to Louisiana, but a little more frayed. They filled the streets with gravel, which wasn't good for the horses or the wagon. Ben found this little hole in the wall place to eat that allowed us ex-slaves to be in. Beta and I kept our heads down and our mouths shut. We didn't know anyone, and we weren't sure how they'd react to new people in town. I had to nurse little George because he was getting fussy. George was going on seven months and catching a fever every other night.

Ben left us eating and went about town, asking questions about places for sale. He had come upon the house selling place and met Mr. Briggs.

"Hello, are you Mr. Briggs, as its stated in the window?"

"Why yes, I am. What can I do for you?" Mr. Briggs asked.

"Good Sir, I am seeking a little place or cottage type home, so I and my family can settle here. I have a new wife and son and her best friend. We come from South Carolina and thought it would be best to move to a less volatile state."

"What is your name, Sir?

"It is Benjamin Henderson."

"Well, Mr. Henderson, we are in a different time and place now, aren't we?" He moved into Ben, and in a lower voice.

"Well, some of the uppity niggers sure have changed things around here."

"Oh, I hope there are some places left around here to purchase?"

"I think I got just the place for you. If you want to look at it, then we can go right now." Mr. Briggs was spry, fat, and just too cheery, with his rosy, red cheeks. "Did you want to bring the misses along?" he asked.

"No. She's nursing our son, and that's something you don't want to disturb. You'll have a screaming baby on your hands."

"Alright then, we can go take a look."

"Give me five minutes to move my wagon and I'll be right back."

"Okay, I'll be waiting right here."

Ben moved the wagon, paid for our meals, and told us to stay in the eatery until he got back. He was gone about two hours when he came back into the eatery. He had just bought a cottage outright, but he wanted to take us to the man he bought it from. When we walked through the door of the property office, Mr. Briggs looked like he had seen a spirit. "Mr. Briggs, here are my wife and child and her best friend. We sure are going to enjoy the home you just sold us. I pray, Sir, your words do not choke you in your sleep this night. We are going to enjoy the house." Mr. Briggs swallowed hard, as though a chicken leg bone was going down. I of course was confused by his reaction. Ben had paid cash and put both our names on the deed. He went with Mr. Briggs to the recorder's office, so they could record it right away. Mr. Briggs didn't want to give the money back, so he went on about his business. It was all more the funnier when we arrived at the home and Ben told me about what Mr. Briggs said. The cottage was all white, with yellow trim and very little furniture. We had to buy new beds and dresser drawers, but everything else was already there. It was an exciting time, as I had bought nothing in a regular store in my life. Joyous with our new lives in Louisiana. It was a Spanish-style cottage, and you could tell the previous owners took care of the place. A pond ran in the back of the house. It was so peaceful. You could hear every sound, every grasshopper, every tree leaf swishing in the wind. The sun shined through the trees and formed angel gowns to let you know they were around.

~

Nakdi took a deep breath. "Nakida, I'm tired now. We can continue tomorrow if that's alright?"

"Sure Nana, that is fine. Tomorrow is Saturday, so I'll come back in the afternoon."

"That'll be fine, baby."

I left Nana unsure about what was to come next in her story. She had smiled the whole time she was talking about the cottage, but when she stopped talking about it, her smile changed just as quick as it came.

When I got back to Nana's the next afternoon, she had been up since five am and finished cooking her soup for dinner. I straightened up her place a bit and found her in the den, sitting on the couch reading her paper.

"Nana are you ready to continue or do you want to wait a little?"

"No child, we can continue." She sat back on the couch.

~

1866, I had Maye that April before and little George was already running around being a big brother. Beta and I had become women that helped the poor families in New Orleans. It was a sad time for many, especially for the Africans, because they had passed laws called Disambiguation (Black codes), which two separate sides were fighting. The Democrats were angry that some local governments weren't following through with discriminatory practices after the Civil War was over.

1865, Ben opened a General Store with the proceeds from the farm his cousin Odell was continuing and the one he started on our land. Beta and I would help the customers in the store, white and African, but we would help the African folks with a lower price and some white's we knew were poor too. Of course, they were sworn to secrecy.

~

"Great-Grandma, you stopped calling the ghosts, ghosts and started calling them white."

"Well, it was a term people were using, I learned. Just as they called us nigger, not African. I don't know why people started calling them ghosts, but that's what they were being called and I only called the ones that were decent white. The mean ones I continued to call ghosts. Do you understand why I called them ghosts?"

"No Nana, I figured you would get around to it."

"I called them ghosts because they were devoid of God's Spirit. They were mean spirits and the way they treated us. They were evil spirits with flesh on them. They were devoid of pigment. It just seemed to fit, and I couldn't think of anything else to call them."

~

Very few knew I was married to Ben, African or White. We had to be very careful. Mr. Briggs, embarrassed at his actions, never spread it around that I was Ben's wife. In 1866, a riot broke out over some laws called the Black Codes. There were very few whites, but they were leading the charge against such codes and a lot of us were there supporting this movement, especially if it was going to help us vote.

*The Union victory in the Civil War may have given some 4 million slaves their freedom, but African Americans faced a new onslaught of obstacles and injustices during the Reconstruction era (1865-1877). By late 1865, when the 13th Amendment officially outlawed the institution of slavery, the question of freed blacks' status in the postwar South was still very much unresolved. Under the lenient Reconstruction policies of President Andrew Johnson, white southerners reestablished civil authority in the former Confederate states in 1865 and 1866. They enacted a series of restrictive laws known as "black codes," which restricted freed blacks' activity and ensured their availability as a labor force now that slavery had been abolished. For instance, many states required blacks to sign yearly labor contracts, if they refused, they risked being arrested as vagrants and fined or forced into unpaid labor. Northern outrage over the black codes helped undermine support for Johnson's policies, and by late 1866, control over Reconstruction had shifted to the more radical wing of the Republican Party in Congress. In the years following the end of Reconstruction, the South reestablished many of the provisions of the black codes as the so-called "Jim Crow laws." These remained firmly in place for almost a century but were finally abolished with the passage of the Civil Rights Act of 1964.*

Access this information for free at:
https://openstax.org/books/us-history/pages/1-introduction

It was on July 30th, of 1866, something I would never forget seeing those men being beaten by officers of the court who were to protect the people. Once again, those ghosts couldn't fathom the thought of anybody being free—other than themselves.

Africans and good white folk were being killed because of the color of the skin and standing up for the former slave. I stood there in the distance holding onto Maye, as Ben was one of the good white folks who were part of the process. We listened to the various men talk about this was going to change history and just in that split second, it had. I ran with Maye in my arms to the first hiding place I could find. There were stairs leading up the side of the doctor's office and I hid there with Maye trembling and afraid some of the evil ghost officers would find us and kill us just because until Ben found us. He had to fight his way through the beating and the killing with Ben Jr. to find me hold up under the stairs. I screamed out his name when I saw him. He grabbed me and held onto me tight, and we ran towards the back of the doctor's office, which was in the opposite direction of where the riot was. When we got to the back of the building, I saw the lady who had taken the *Weaving Basket*. I stopped cold in my tracks to look at her. She looked at me also, frightened, and scared, and her eyes pierced through mine, but it wasn't because she recognized me. It was because her husband had been at that convention meeting as well. Ben tugged on me for us to get away and get back to the store. We stayed there until it was safe to go back out again. I was in shock, and it wasn't because of the riot, well that had a little to do with it.

After all the bloodshed had ended, Ben went out and spoke to the other business owners and I then talked to Beta.

"Beta, I saw the lady who took the *Weaving Basket*."

"What weaving basket are you talking about?"

"The weaving basket that had Ms. Susie's baby in it. I saw her today! She was behind the doctor's office. She saw me, and she looked scared out of her mind about the riot going on, but she didn't recognize me. I recognized her, though. What is she doing here in Vieux Carre'?"

"I don't know Nakdi, but if she's here, then the weaving basket is here, too. Why do I keep saying weaving basket? That boy is here too Nakdi."

"I didn't see any children with her. She was coming out of the doctor's office. I wonder if she's married to the doctor?"

"It may be best Nakdi if we ask around town. Since, she doesn't know us, we may talk to her. We can tell her we're from South Carolina and you recognized her from seeing her around town to see what she says. Somehow, we have to find out if that boy is here."

"Beta, what are we going to do if he is?"

"We are just going to keep our mouths shut. Lord have mercy on us. Of all the places they could have come, they had to come here too."

Ben came back into the store, reassuring us everything was alright, but it wasn't in our eyes. I didn't know why it bothered me so much to see her. If she didn't know us, then we had nothing to worry about. Even though things had calmed down and they inspired change, it killed people, equality was far away, and we knew we'd never see it in our lifetime.

~

Seventeen years later, in 1883, our little Maye was about to graduate from school and was going off to college. George went to engineering school, and we had one more left, Samuel, who would turn fourteen.

Five years prior, Beta found love with a man named Christopher Henry and they moved to Chicago. We wrote each other letters every month. I expected her letters, just as she had expected mine. Ben had such success with the store, he started another agricultural farm and allowed students to come there and learn during the time they were not in school. Some would come during seeding time to study how long it would take from planting until a bud of life would show through the ground. I always thought it was boring and fascinating. Boring that they would be out there studying and watching and looking each day, but fascinating, they didn't seem to mind there was black and white alike doing the same thing. It had been his success that drew students and unmentionable men to our doorstep. Ben would ask me about my first impressions of some men who wanted to work on the farm. Most was okay, but few I had to tell him to turn them away. Each time, I had to pretend I was of service to the house and not Ben's wife when ghosts would come around looking for work and their conversation was that we were still slaves or servants of the home to them.

It was hot out one summer day when one came by to see about work. Ben was at the store and, being the hospitable person, I showed him around the farm and offered him something to drink. I made him stand outside while I retrieved his lemonade and we talked for another few minutes after finishing his drink.

"Is the owner of this farm in today?" the man said.

"No, he is off at the store, but I'll let him know you stopped by. Can you come by another day, say tomorrow? He should be here all day." I said. He had been a perfect gentleman until that point, and then it turned ugly. He grabbed my arm and put a knife up against my side and told me to not say a word or he would kill me where I stood.

"You got any money in here?"

"No, I don't keep money here. Massa Ben, keep all the money with him."

I had reverted to be a slave to stay alive. Once he found there was no money to be had, he turned his attentions to taking my body for however long he needed. I was thankful at that moment my children were not present. He had thrown me down on the ground and started pulling my up dress when I saw his body swing upward and his feet were dangling off the floor. Franklin, a tall African man hired two weeks prior to help on the farm, saw what had taken place at the door. Franklin moved in and grabbed the fellow by the back of his shirt and grabbed the knife out of his hand and handed it to me. My first impulse was to stab him with it and do him like they had done to Mr. Willie, but I asked Franklin to tie him up and we would take him to the law. Of course, he was out in a few days, but the judge told him to get out of town and never come back. No, justice wasn't fair, because he was a ghost, but at least we would never see him again. Ben was grateful. There was nothing he wouldn't do for Franklin. Franklin had been a bounty hunter and law man in another life. He wanted somewhere quiet he could work and be free to live and he found that freedom on our farm. Franklin had no wife or children or other family alive he would talk about. He had become my protector when Ben wasn't around. Often, he would talk about where he came from in Mississippi. He wasn't so lucky at the beginning of his life, as we was slashed on the back by the whips of his master. He got free doing the bounty work and he was good at it. He soon lost the taste for it once he knew he was free to do what he wanted after the war. The man he worked for gave him his papers of freedom and then he died a month later.

~

The next day, I went out to the mailbox, looking for a letter from Beta, and found a letter from the South Carolina State Mental Hospital addressed to Ben. I ran it over to him as fast as I could muster. When I reached him, I was out of breath and scared of what the letter might say.

"Nakdi, what's going on? Why did you run all the way here?" Ben asked. Unable to speak from being out of breath. I just handed him the letter. I stared him in the face breathing hard the whole time he opened it and read the letter.

"It looks like I'm going to take a trip to Carolina. Susie is being released. She has no family left out there to take care of her."

"You mean after all this time. They're going to let her out. Is she well enough to be let out?"

"I don't know Nakdi. I don't know what's going on, but they are releasing her in two weeks."

"Then I have to go with you."

"Nakdi, Samuel and Maye are still in school, and I need you to watch the store."

"Ben, you needed me when you took her to the hospital. You don't think you need me now?" I asked. He saw my frustration at what he was saying, but I don't think he knew what I was thinking.

"Nakdi, I love you and only you. We will be together for the rest of our lives. I'm not going back to South Carolina to stay. I'm going to make sure Susie is okay and I can find her a place to live."

"Ben!"

He put his finger up and kissed me. I realized how little he knew me and how much he was listening to others about how to treat their wives. He thought I was jealous about Susie being let out of the hospital and the thought of him rushing back into her arms again was the farthest thing from my mind. I looked him dead in his face and said, "Okay." I turned towards the door and walked away and didn't say another word about it.

I got home, packed some of his belongings. Enough for at least a week. I cooked supper in the evening. Maye and Samuel ate, and they retired to their rooms to study. Ben came in during the early part of the evening. I made his plate, and we sat at the dinner table to eat together. I was quiet and didn't want to pick a fight, but I had to speak. "Ben, after supper, I would like to speak to you about this trip to South Carolina." He said okay, and we ate in silence.

He cleared our dishes and washed them and put them away. I found him in the study, reading some of his agricultural material. "Ben Henderson." He looked up at me and could tell we were going to have a serious discussion. I did not sit, but I stood near the fireplace and stared at him. Would he understand my point in this matter or would he brush it off like it didn't matter, because his point was more important than mine? So, I spoke, "After your comments today, I realized after all this time, you don't know me at all deep down inside. I am no longer that eighteen-year-old girl needing your protection, so long ago. Nor am I a woman to be jealous of another. I was never jealous of Ms. Susie then, nor will I be now. So, I have packed a week's worth of clothing and will pack whatever you else you may need for the trip to South Carolina. You do what you feel you need to do for Ms. Susie, and you get back to your family as soon as possible. And know this Benjamin, as much as you have fought for our love to be free to the world, you have set our relationship back a hundred years. I know every inch of you. I know when you're upset and worried about something because your breathing is different. I know when you want to make love to me and when you don't want to be bothered. I know when another woman gets your attention, because I have studied you, Benjamin Henderson. I have studied the very man who is brilliant at farming and helping people, but you have lacked in studying me and who I am as a person. Your wife and the mother of your children. If you don't get out of your own way, you will be lost and there's nothing I can do to help you. I will be in our bedroom waiting for you." I walked out of the room and prepared myself for bed. Standing at my dresser, he came into the room and walked up behind me. He had caressed me like he had done for the first time twenty years ago. I turned to him, and he saw the necklace he had given me so long ago. There was no more talk about jealousy ever again.

# 7

## *The Weaving Basket Comes Home to Roost*

Ben was off to South Carolina the next morning. I left for the store after the children had gone to school. Once there, he sent me a telegram of his arrival and that he loved me and the children. It was already October and at this point, the weather was unpredictable.

Ben arrived at the farm and the next day, went to the hospital to talk to the doctor about Ms. Susie. Dr. Freedman met with Ben to discuss her plight and discharge. He expressed Dr. Porter died a few years back and Dr. Freedman oversaw her care.

"Mr. Henderson, Susie is in and out of reality. Her mind is stuck in 1857, when she was married to you. She can cook and clean and is no longer a danger to herself or to others. In all honesty, we need the bed for someone who is sicker than she is. As you know, her parents are deceased."

"Actually, no. I didn't know. I haven't been in Carolina for over twenty years."

"She has no other relatives to take her in. From her file, I know you are no longer married to Ms. Cobalt, but we have no one else to turn to. If someone doesn't take her, she will end up on the streets. Times have changed, Mr. Henderson. Compassion for people is gone with the new state regulations in place now. I would like for you to see her today and talk with her so you will get an understanding of where her mind is. I would like for you to come as often as you can, so she can get used to you again, until we release her on Sunday."

"Mr. Freedman, I will do what I can for her."

"I know it will be a difficult transition, but I want you to ease her into the reality that your lives have changed. If you do that, I think her mind's transition will be a much smoother process."

In the halls, Ben expressed things had changed in the hospital. No one walked the halls babbling to themselves and it was much quieter than his last visit there. Ben followed Dr. Freedman and let him into her room.

Susie turned to him, "Benjamin, what happened to you. You've aged so much. Life has stressed you so?"

"Well, working on the farm and taking care of everything is a lot for one person."

"Oh well, with me back, I'll be able to help. Did Dr. Freedman tell you I leave here on Sunday?"

"Why yes Susie, he did and I'm sure you will be a big help on the farm. A lot of things have changed. I can't wait for you to see the recent changes that have taken place. It's an exciting time."

Benjamin went into an awkward silence. "Yes, Dr. Freedman told me there were a lot of changes that took place in South Carolina, and it may shock me, but take everything in and use my coping skills and techniques as they taught me. He said I should be able to get back into the rhythm of things at home."

Dr. Freedman shook his head at Ben, as to say, 'don't break it to her right now.' This is one of those situations where she needs to be eased into reality.

"I just wanted you to know I will come to see you and pick you up to take you home on Sunday."

"Will Nakdi be with you? You know she will need to pack up my things and carry them to the carriage for me."

"Susie, Nakdi won't be with me. I'll tell you all about everything when I see you again and when we get home. I need you to pack your own belongings." Susie gasped and put her hands up to her cheeks.

"You haven't sold Nakdi, have you?"

"No." he said.

Ms. Susie grabbed his neck and kissed him, as though they had never parted, and then turned and got into her bed as though Benjamin had never been there. She didn't say goodbye. He didn't exist.

~

"Nakida, as much as your great grandpa thought he knew me, I knew him better. I knew he wouldn't be able to handle this situation on his own. He was a brilliant farmer and business owner, but in emotional ties and relationships, he had no clue of what to do."

"Nana, I don't know too much about relationships and the complexities of the brain, but couldn't she go back to being more deeply crazy in the head once she found out he was no longer married to her and instead married to you?"

"You see. He didn't quite tell her himself."

~

Ben brought Ms. Susie to the Henderson Farm. They stayed there a week with his cousins, and not once did he mention to her they weren't married anymore. She wasn't well enough to ask the questions, and they would not rock the boat. The only thing he explained to her was he didn't live there anymore and would leave for Louisiana next week and his expectation was to leave her there at the Henderson Farm.

During that week, she became friendly with Rudy again and Ben didn't know how to handle that situation and he used it as an excuse to bring her down to Vieux Carre'. Ben sent me a telegram letting me know when he would leave from South Carolina, but never once mentioned to me he was bringing Susie with him. He knew I'd protest the idea, but what could I do?

~

When they arrived at our home, it was early in the morning, so the children were gone to school. I saw the wagon coming, and I ran outside the house to greet Ben, to hug and to kiss him and to love all over him, because I missed him so. I ran around the carriage. The door opens and there Ms. Susie came stepping out.

"Oh Nakdi, I am so happy to see you. How have you been? I'm glad you came with Ben to take care of him, while I was away in the hospital. Come here gal, help me get my things and take me to our room." She grabbed my hand like she did when she owned me. My blood boiled and I snatched it from her. Ben had taken the carriage inside the barn and when he walked around the bend of the house, he saw my face and stopped in his tracks.

"Ben, bring the bags into our bedroom, so I can tell Nakdi about the trip down here. She's acting a little funny today. You need to talk with her."

"I will do that right away. Honey, can you…." I stared at him again and his speech stopped dead in mid-sentence. I turned to Ms. Susie.

"Ms. Susie, I am going to show you to your room, and you can unpack your things. I am going to come out to the barn and help Ben…."

"Excuse me gal. When have you been given the right to just call him Ben? He is Master Ben to you and don't you ever forget it." Her hand went up to slap me and Ben saw me make a fist. He stepped in between us. Ben had his back turned to Ms. Susie and was facing me.

"Ms. Susie, why don't I take you to the room we have for you and then I'll help Nakdi with the horses. You need your rest and then we'll wake you when lunch is ready."

"That's quite fine, but later I want to catch up with Nakdi. You are going to teach me a thing or two about this place."

I walked away to the barn without saying a word. My pounding head was about to explode. I guess he was learning about me now. I went to the barn to see my Misty. He had taken my horse on the trip.

When Ben came into the barn, he came up behind me and started apologizing and begging me not to hate him, and he could explain everything.

"Benjamin Henderson, there is no need to explain anything, but let me tell you what we're going to do. After lunch, we will sit Ms. Susie down and tell her everything and we will allow her to process the information as best as she can. I know you didn't have the heart to tell her you weren't married to her anymore. I know you couldn't bear the responsibility of making her sicker than what she already is. But let's be clear about a few things. One, we will tell her you are not married to her anymore and I'm not her maid and we have three beautiful children together. Two, she is a guest in our home, and she is welcome to stay here until the day she dies, but I will not be the owned Nakdi with her and she will pull her weight around here as well. And three, Benjamin Henderson, if you ever pull a stunt like this again, you won't be able to imagine what I can do to you in your sleep. I love you with every part of my being Mr. Henderson, but if she can't handle what we are going to tell her, then we will find somewhere else for her to live, and you will pay for it. Those are my conditions and right now, all you need to do is, agree."

"I agree with everything you have said, if I can kiss the love of my life." We made love in the barn. I lay there, looking at his face.

"Nakdi, I'm sorry I didn't tell you she was coming. I didn't know what to do. One minute she was herself and the next, she was flirting with Rudy. I couldn't take the chance on leaving her there and something happens to her." He didn't see my expression change, but it did.

"Plus, I felt responsible." he said.

"Ben, I know you feel responsible for her, and I get it, I do, but you can't put our lives and our relationship on hold while you are trying to save Ms. Susie. Her mind doesn't process like a normal mind does. When we tell her, be prepared, she may lose it again. If she does, then we should find a place for her out here. I won't live like a slave in my home, and I don't want her to be a problem for the children."

"I know. Let's just see how the talk goes." I lay there on the haystack with Ben for another twenty minutes, contemplating the worst that could happen. Does she lose it and try to kill us all or herself? Does she go into deep depression and never return? After all this time, would she take the news well enough to stay sane?

I fixed lunch, and Ben went to wake Susie up from her nap. Ben sat at one end of the table, and Susie sat at the other. I guess she didn't mind too much. I didn't want to hear anymore slavery talk, so I ate my lunch in the kitchen like I used to. Lunch was finished. We all sat in the living room area, where we told Ms. Susie about everything. It was a blur of ramblings to which she sat and listened. The noise of the blur was even quieter and then she looked at me. Her eyes pierced through me, just like the weaving basket's mother had.

"Where is my baby?"

"Ms. Susie, both babies died during the war." I said.

"I'm not talking about those dead babies. I'm talking about the baby I had with Rudy. Nakdi, you and Beta took him from me, and I want to know where my baby is?" Ben looked at me, and then I looked back at Ms. Susie. A part of me wanted to believe she said what she said to get back at me, but how could she know Ben didn't know about the Weaving Basket.

"We had to give the weaving basket away. We had to get him off the plantation, because Mr. Willie would have killed him if he knew you had a baby with Rudy, and it lived." Ben walked out of the room and headed out to the field. I sat down next to Ms. Susie and told her what happened to the weaving basket. "We wanted to keep him near. I would have claimed him for myself, but nobody would have ever believed me, and we were sure the baby wouldn't survive if the men on the plantation found out. We didn't name him, because we didn't want to get too attached, but how could we not even for that bit of time we had him with us. We took him to the doctor's office and left him there. A woman got him and loved on him the first time she saw him, and we knew he was in excellent hands. I cried tears of joy for the weaving basket, because he would be free, Ms. Susie."

"Nakdi, thank you for saving my baby. I'm going to lie down now."

I saw sad and happy in her eyes all at once. She had sunk into deeper non-reality in just a split second of time from one to the other, but she had remembered giving birth to Rudy's child.

A while later, Maye and Samuel came in from school. I had to sit them down and tell them about Ms. Susie and all that had transpired that afternoon. Samuel had gone out to the field to talk to Ben and Maye stayed with me to start dinner and to look after Ms. Susie. With what I had told them, Maye had filled her heart with compassion for Ms. Susie without even meeting her.

The children met Ms. Susie during supper time, and they played games together outside in the yard and talked some more. I watched them from the kitchen window as the sun set for the night and they couldn't see. Telling them all to come in was talking to three five-year-old children. It would be Saturday on tomorrow, they could talk to Ms. Susie more then.

I knew it hurt Ben to hear the news, but what could he do about it now. He was already in bed when I came into the room. He was sitting up, waiting for me. When I get into the bed, he asked me the question.

"Is it true?" he asked.

"Yes. When you left the second time to go fight in the war, Susie had lost it. She would stay in her bed for weeks at a time. Other days, she would feel good enough to walk around the farm and take care of herself, even though we knew the challenges in her head. It wasn't often she could get out of bed. On the day, she gave birth to the baby, she was screaming so loud, we thought her insides were coming out. She was not showing like a regular woman shows when they are pregnant, and it seemed like the last couple of months, she just laid there out of herself. I ran to her bedside to check to see what was wrong, and I saw the baby's head. Beta and I hid the baby for months until we could get him off the plantation and leave him somewhere somebody could find him and take care of him. I didn't even realize who the daddy was until you came home and was trying to get Ms. Susie to recognize you. You didn't notice because you were in your own grief, but she would stare out the window for hours looking at Rudy and he would do the same while he was working in the yard area around the house. We knew neither one of them could take care of that child. Ms. Susie was not in reality, and Rudy was born touched as well, but their connection we could not figure out. It was love in its rarest form. We could not keep the child on the farm with you coming home. We knew if Mr. Willie or you found out about the baby, you'd killed all three of them and lost your mind too. Why because that baby lived from her womb and your babies with Ms. Susie didn't. I did what was right in the sight of God and if I had to do over again, I wouldn't change a thing." He was not looking at me. "Ben, look at me." He turned to look me in the eye. "I never meant for you to find out this way, but it's something that happened a long time ago. You can't hold on to the past, just like I haven't. You should leave Ms. Susie, Rudy, and that boy in the past. I am the one with you here now. We have three beautiful children together. Don't let this situation tare us apart. You can't let it."

"I know Nakdi, and I won't. It's just the whole thing is shocking, and I'm confused about why you kept this from me all these years."

"In your state of mind, when you came back from the war, you wouldn't have been able to think straight. Would you have been able to make a rash decision about the situation? You left her alone to fight in a war who had no winners, because my people are not free. You didn't come back the same man who left two separate occasions to fight in a war. I know deep down inside you didn't want to fight, but you did, because you had to make sure the townspeople didn't turn on you. You were our slave, Master. I wasn't thinking about your feelings. I was thinking about three people's lives in the balance. If I wanted true revenge on Ms. Susie, I would have told you. If you had gotten any wind of the fact someone had Ms. Susie and for the record, even though he was a simple man, Rudy loved her more than you did. He loved her like you are to love me. He loved her, Ben, because you didn't, and the guilt is going to eat you alive if you don't let the past go. I love you no matter the circumstance. Can you do the same?"

He pulled me close. "Nakdi, I love you, and that will never change. I just know now it was a mistake bringing her here. I need to take her back or bring Rudy here, so they can be together. To be honest, I got a little jealous she was spending time with him after they released her from the hospital. I want her to be happy and at least he can keep her occupied."

We laughed and talked a bit more and then he asked the most frightening question, "Huh, that it very curious. I wonder whatever happened to Mr. Willie?"

My heart started beating out of rhythm. "I don't know. One day he was there and the next, he was gone."

He kissed me goodnight, and we went off to sleep. There was no way I was going to say what happened to Mr. Willie. That secret would go with me to the grave.

# 8

# *The Rudy Effect*

The household was stirring early the next morning. I curled over and slapped Ben in the head by accident.

"Okay, I'm up, I'm up." Ben sat straight up in the bed.

"What happened?" he asked. "You punched me in the head."

"I am sorry. I smelled breakfast, and I thought it was you cooking." We both at the same time ran down the stairs to make sure Susie was not about to burn the house down. We run to the kitchen, and it was Maye. She was seventeen going on eighteen now and all grown up. We strolled in together. Not wanting to appear worried at what she was doing.

"Everything smells wonderful." I told her.

"Thanks mom. Can you wake up Samuel and Auntie Susie? I will serve breakfast shortly."

Ben and I shuffled out of the kitchen. He assumed nothing of it, but I knew Maye well and something was up. She learned to cook with me, but never cooked breakfast on her own. Maye was buttering us up for the slaughter.

"Ben, your daughter is up to something, and this breakfast is for us to let her have her way."

"It could be she is trying to do a kind gesture." Ben suggested.

"Knowing how your child's mind works is a mother's duty. Watch and learn."

With breakfast finished, Maye asks us to remain behind. "Maye, what is this all about?" Ben asked as a worried father. He had plunged to the correct verdict, but he didn't know it yet.

"Well, I'm in love with a boy. I mean, he's not a boy. He's not too old. He's twenty-one."

Ben does all the talking and doesn't allow me to get a word in edge wise. I could see it in her eyes. She had fallen hard.

"Well, tell us about this boy-man, because you have never mentioned him before now."

She beams. "His name is Nigel Brackett, and he just turned twenty-one. He also goes to George's school."

I didn't know why, but I had such a comfort at that moment. I heard Brackett come out of her mouth. I could go back to tuning in to my daughter speak about her love and I could observe Ben interrogate her in tranquility.

"Nigel is in the Engineering program, just like George. That's how we met. George came to see me at school and then they came by the General Store."

"So, when do we get to meet the love of your life, because neither you nor your brother have mentioned him? I would like to meet the young man my daughter is so smitten over."

"Father, please don't be too hard on him. He comes from a wonderful family, and I know you're going to love him. Can he come by for supper tomorrow? He and George is coming home for the summer today!"

Because Ben was contemplating the question of allowing this young man to come for supper tomorrow, I got my say in, "Maye, we love you so much and we want you to be happy and find love and if this boy makes you happy, then yes, we would love to meet him tomorrow for supper. We will talk more after we meet him and, your father won't scare him off."

She hugs Ben for dear life. She was a daddy's girl. He spoiled her rotten and she could do no wrong, even though she hadn't given us any reason not to trust her judgement. I wanted to wait and see.

Maye was attractive with Sandy Blond hair, like all my children, with hazel eyes. If I couldn't share my love so true with the world without being judged for it, then I certainly would not hide who my children were. Their own culture talked about them, and the ghosts from slavery's past didn't want to know the truth about who they were from the inception of life. These ghosts were a part of humanity. Their existence was real. They bled just like we did, but it wasn't just because they were void of pigment that I called them ghosts. It was because they were void of what God had designed them to be, faithful human souls. They were void of knowing the worth of other human beings who were not like them in color only. They were void of the existence of truth. We fought for our children to never feel secondary to anybody. They were African and White children to the world, but we taught them to embrace who they were inside and out.

That afternoon, our George arrived home and all he could do was talk about school and what he was researching, but it was our mission to find out about this fellow, Nigel Brackett.

"Your sister is seeking to influence my mind about this Nigel Brackett. Tell us about him."

"She was ever the spoiled one, wasn't she? Father, you never knew how to say no to her."

"She's my only daughter," Ben got defensive. "I have to set the model for the husband she will marry one day."

George put his hand on his father's shoulder. "Nigel is a great guy. He's smart and gifted. We are roommates. That's how Maye, met him. About five months ago, we came to her school and then to the General Store, while she was working there. They locked onto each other and they've been corresponding ever since. He comes down to see her every Saturday at the Library. It's sickening. All he talks about is Maye. What don't I understand is why you both are just now hearing about him?"

I hadn't thought about it until George mentioned it. "She has been keeping him a secret. We didn't know she was so smitten with anyone, but now it makes sense with the library visits every Saturday. We didn't know she was so serious about any boy. So, what does he look like?"

"He's no different from us. I've met his parents twice, and they seem to have a loving relationship. He talks about them all the time, other than Maye. Anyway, you'll have time to meet him on tomorrow. Can I excuse myself from the table now? I have to unpack."

"Sure son. Tell Maye to check in on Ms. Susie," Ben said.

"Who's Ms. Susie?"

I mushed my cheeks between my hands. We had forgotten to tell George about Ms. Susie and her living with us. I hugged him and told him once he got settled, to come back down and we would tell him all about her.

~

"Nakida, I think I'm done for the day."

"No problem, Nana. I don't want to wear you out. Eat something and then relax. I'm off tomorrow and Monday from school. You want me to come back on Monday to give you a day's rest?"

"Sure, baby, that would be nice. I have church service on tomorrow."

"I love you, Nana. You make sure you get some rest, okay."

"I will. You don't worry about me. You go, and I will see you on Monday."

It was already eight o'clock at night. I sat on the bus hoping I could rest myself, because my mind was running a thousand miles per hour. My Nana was still alive, and she lived through so much, but I knew her story had more to reveal.

Monday, around eleven, Nana was up cleaning and cooking. I talked to her for a while about how school was going and my personal life, which was non-existent. I didn't have the time or the energy for a relationship. For the next hour, we both napped, but I slept longer than she did. I woke up around one-thirty in the afternoon and smelled food cooking. I laid there long enough until she came out of the kitchen on her own. She had that old lady waddle, but it was cute to witness. Life so wore her six-foot frame down a bit, but I knew my Nana was strong and could be around if she needed to be.

"Nakida, I'm ready to continue if you are? I saw you were sleeping so peaceful. I didn't want to wake you."

"It's okay Nana. The smell of those greens and cornbread woke me."

"You know I have some white bean soup going too. If you want to stay for dinner, you can."

"Nana, I would love to. I haven't had your cooking in a while now. Also, I'm shocked you didn't call them ghost beans." We both laughed, and then she sat down to continue.

"I might even finish my story by tonight, but we'll see how it goes."

"Take your time Nana."

"You know your great grandpa loved my cooking."

"I do too Nana, I do too."

"You know it would be many days when he would come in from working the store or the farm starving. Sometimes Ben wouldn't eat all day because of work, or I'd tell him what I would cook for supper, and he wouldn't eat until he got home." My Nana laughed with the most joyful laugh.

~

That evening, George Jr. came down. He had gotten a little of the story about Ms. Susie from Maye, but we had to give him the details about what was going on and we talked until midnight telling him everything after meeting her during supper.

Sunday, Maye was preparing and worrying about our meeting with Nigel for the first time. She was as jittery as a firefly and cried a few times. When we returned from church service, Nigel would be there by noon. She wanted everything fancy and perfect and nice, which I was never one to be proper and fancy. I didn't know where she got her traits from, but I knew she never got them from me. Maybe Ms. Susie was brushing off on her. All I wanted was to meet this Nigel and find out his intentions for my daughter. I guess Ben's idea was to scare him to death. When he came through the door, Maye was smiling from ear-to-ear. Ben shook his hand and George greeted him like he had always done and me. I fainted. When I woke up, I was laying in my bed asking what happened.

"Nakdi, you fainted. Are you alright?" Ben asked.

"Yes, I'm fine. At least I think I'm fine. Maybe, it was the heat today." Maye was sitting on the side of the bed, holding my hand, looking scared. "I'm fine Maye. I overworked myself. You go back to your guest. Your father can interrogate him for me. Let Nigel know I am so sorry and will properly greet him the next time he comes. Maybe, he can come back tomorrow, and I'll meet him then."

"I think right now, you need to rest." Ben said.

"I will Ben. Both of you go down. I should be fine." Ben grabbed my hand and then kissed me as Maye was walking out the door. I assured Ben I would be fine and if I needed anything, I would let them know. Once Ben left the room, I cried uncontrollably. Could our lives get any more complicated? When Nigel walked through the door, all I could see was Rudy.

~

"Oh! My goodness Nana! Are you serious?" Nakida said.

"Baby, my life was spiraling. If he wasn't, then I knew I was going crazy."

~

After crying so much, I thought I was seeing things, or maybe I was just imagining it. Through all my crying and wondering, Samuel came in to check on me and to report on Ms. Susie. She had become his project.

"Momma, Ms. Susie, keeps calling me Rudy. She keeps saying, 'Is that you Rudy?' when I walk through the door. When I get closer to her, then she says, *'No, you are not my Rudy.'* It's a little weird."

"I know, son, but she doesn't mean any harm. She's just remembering someone she loved when she was in Carolina. One day, you will grow up and fall in love like that, too. Guess what, I think your sister is in love like that."

"Mom, I don't know about all that love stuff. Right now, I'm just trying to get through school without being picked on."

"Well, tell me how I can help you and I'll try my best." I said to Samuel. He was my baby boy. He was sweat and kind. Samuel never gave us any trouble at all.

"Right now, everything is wonderful. We're on break and I'll have some time to come up with some strategies." I kissed him goodbye, and he was off. I went back to thinking about Nigel and what I saw may not have been what I saw.

After Nigel left, Ben came in to check on me, too. "I need to know what's going on with you, Nakdi?"

Tears roll down my face. Ben wiped them away. "Is Nigel gone?" I asked him.

"Yes. George, Maye, and Nigel went into town. What's going on?"

"I...I think Nigel is Rudy and Susie's son. When he walked in the door, all I saw was Rudy."

"Nakdi, how can you be so sure he's theirs?" Ben asked.

"Ben, I worked with and saw Rudy every day. We were the same age as when I came to Henderson. Maybe, I am jumping to conclusion, or I am imagining the whole thing, but having all this stress is taking a toll on me. My gut is telling me I'm not crazy. I can't ask him. He may not know the answers. Only his parents can provide the right information."

"If we find out he is Rudy and Susie's son, it wouldn't be so bad, would it?" Ben asked.

"It's not so much the fact he will find out about his actual parents, but what about Maye? This is the first time she's fallen for a boy. She may not take this situation well. The fact he's the son of Ms. Susie. Does the psychological thing pass down to the children?"

"Not to be the only voice of reason here, but I hope we've raised our daughter to be strong like her mother and we all will get through this together. They are not blood related, so that shouldn't be a problem. I don't know if mental illness is hereditary or not. The problem may be Nigel's parents. We don't know if they told him they found him in Carolina. They may not have wanted him to know who his birth parents are."

"It's the past Ben I'm worried about. Once we open this bucket of reality, then you know all the questions will come. Especially if Nigel wants to know all the details of his existence. We won't have the right to keep it from him. We need to speak to Nigel's parents and see what they say without him knowing anything, and we can't tell Maye either for now. Ben, I need you to get as much information out of George as soon as possible to see if we can get Nigel's parents out here for a visit. We can't hold on to this too much longer. My nerves can't take it. I wish Beta was here."

"Nakdi," Ben said, worried.

Maybe I had hurt his feelings by saying I wanted Beta there. He didn't say, but I think Ben worried about me becoming like Ms. Susie. This scared him, and I could see it. I don't think he could handle that happening again.

~

"Your great grandpa was a worrier most times. We had gone through so much throughout the years, I was wondering if our relationship would survive one more thing. I didn't know how this situation was going to turn out, but I was hoping it would be the last thing we had to tend to. It was the last thing hanging over my head."

"Nana, I mean you know how it all turned out in the end after all this time, but what if it wasn't Mr. Rudy's and Ms. Susie's son? You had stressed yourself out for nothing."

"I know, but you need to know something about me, Nakida. After all that time and even now, my gut never lies. It wasn't so much about me, but it was Nigel and Maye."

~

It would be a month before we could get his parents out to our home. I didn't want to be shocked at what I saw, so I stayed in the house and let everyone meet each other and then I would enter. Of course, I was never one for dramatics, so when Beta showed up that morning with her husband, I was sure it was going to be one strange day. Lease it to say, before I could even tell her about Susie, she walked into the room she used to sleep in. I followed behind her, I knew a scream was coming. Who was it going to be first? This time, the scream came from Susie, because of her being naked and all, and Beta just busted through the door. 'Beta, what are you doing here?' Susie yelled.

Stopping in my tracks and waiting for Beta to come out of the room into the hall, her look was an unbelievable shock. "Beta let me explain why she is here." Susie slammed the door and didn't come out for the rest of the day. "Beta come to the sitting area and I'll tell you everything." It took me two hours to explain and by the time I finished, Nigel's parents were here, and I held onto Beta's hand in order not to fall apart. We stood there near the front entrance and all I could see was her standing there next to one of the most handsome African men I had ever seen. Squeezing Beta's hand, I almost cut off the circulation and nearly broke her fingers. Ben led them to through the entryway and I stood there to greet them and was in utter shock at who was coming in. When the Doctor's wife, so we thought, came in, she looked at me as though her eyes were piercing through me again. We all walked into the sitting room and there was silence for two minutes. It could have been five, but I didn't know the full extent of time that passed. It was Nigel and Maye who began speaking and introducing everyone. There were no words coming out until I realized everyone was staring at me. "Ah, Maye, please get everyone a refreshing drink dear." Maye got up, and Nigel got up and followed behind her.

In the kitchen, they couldn't help but wonder. "Something funny is going on here. My mother has been acting strange ever since you came here the last time."

"Do you think it's the suddenness of our relationship? I mean, they're just now finding out about us. I hope your mother doesn't faint again."

"Nigel, I don't know what's going on, but I am going to make it my business to find out." Maye said, "Right now, we can't ask too many questions. Our parents are meeting for the first time."

"I wonder if it surprised your mother my father is African, and my mother is white?"

"That should be the last thing that should bother her. She hasn't said too much to me at all since you first met her."

"Maye, we can't get all excited about this. We must show we are mature enough to be in this relationship. So, let's get back in there with the drinks." Both returning with big fake grins on their faces and drinks in hand.

"So, Mr. and Mrs. Brackett, our children are in love, and they want our permission to continue to see each other. What are your thoughts about this?" Ben asked.

Mr. Brackett speaks. "Maye is a lovely girl, and we were just as surprised at their relationship as you were. Nigel let us know a few weeks ago," Mr. Brackett, then let out a giggle.

The tension in the air seemed unbearable. We filled the room with the thickness of anxiety. Nakdi stood and asked for Nigel, Maye, and George to leave the room. "The married adults would like some time to speak and get to know each other."

All looked and smiled at their parents. "Sure mom," George stated, "Come and get us when you are ready." They walked out of the sitting area. "We will George."

After leaving the room, they went outside to talk. "I don't know what's going on in there, but I have never seen my mother act this way around anyone before." George said.

"It's scaring me a little." Maye wanted to break down crying, she later told me. Nigel grabbed her and hugged her, saying, "Don't worry about a thing." George turned to Nigel and asked if he was okay, "You are sweating."

"Yes, I am a little nervous. It's just my future with Maye is important to me and I want our parents' approval, but it won't mean if they disapprove, I'm going to stop seeing her. That's just not going to happen. I don't want our foundation starting off on the wrong foot." Maye grabs Nigel's hand. They were all looking worried now, and they had no clue why.

In the house, Nakdi was fidgeting. Nigel's mother got up and walked over to me. She grabbed my hands and looked at me with those piercing eyes again, but this time I could see the sincerity of her stare. It was as if they begged me to open my mouth and it obliged.

"Ben and I are from South Carolina."

"So are we. We moved here a year after the war ended." Mrs. Brackett said.

"I was wondering if you knew Dr. Porter."

"Why yes, he's, my father. I worked at his office often. I don't remember seeing you there as a patient."

"Back then, I was a slave and Dr. Porter would come to the Henderson Plantation on house calls."

"Thank the good Lord above you got out of that godforsaken place."

"I guess so." I said. She continued to hold my hands.

"Well, my husband and I met here in Vieux Carre'. I recognize you from when the riot broke out. You were carrying a child, and I saw Mr. Henderson trying to get you out of there. Oh! Mr. Henderson weren't you the owner of that plantation in South Carolina?"

Ben had not wanted to bring up the past, but it was never far behind. "Yes, my father was the owner. I took over before his death. I am not proud of that fact, but I could make some changes of my own after the war was over." Nakdi wanted to save Ben at this point. "Yes, he made substantial changes. I also remember the day of the riot. You seemed terrified. I recognized you, but you didn't recognize me."

"Well, how did you know it was me for sure? I never went with my father to the plantations." Ben interjected at this point.

"Nakdi, do you think we need to freshen up their lemonade?"

Looking at Ben so caring, he looked at me the same with the most understanding eyes. "I remember you Mrs. Brackett, because you were the one who found the baby boy where I left him, which was next to Dr. Porter's steps at the back of his office."

Mrs. Brackett dropped tears like raindrops falling out of the trees in Africa where I would play. Her glass would have dropped as well, if her husband had not grabbed it in time, as it was about to shake to the floor.

"Oh, my God, he's your son!"

"No, no, Mrs. Brackett. Nigel is not mine or Ben's son." Nakdi caught her breath as Mr. Brackett continued to console his wife.

"I think you better sit down, because I have to tell you the complete story."

After two hours of telling the entire story again, no one could hold back the tears. Ben spoke at that point. "I know my wife has given you both a lot to deal with today, but we both want you to know we will respect your wishes and hold this information if you never want Nigel to know who his birth parents are."

Mrs. Brackett stood up and asked, "May I meet Miss Susie?" Mr. Brackett asked if that was what she wanted to do? "I want to meet her John." He looked at Ben and nodded with the assurance everything was going to be alright. Ben went to get Ms. Susie and when they walked into the sitting room, Susie went into theatrics.

"My, my, my, we're having a party. Why didn't someone tell me we were having a party, Ben?"

"Susie, we're not having a party. We are meeting Nigel's parents for the first time and when we told her you were from South Carolina, she wanted to meet you."

"Oh, how lovely? It's so nice to meet you. Please excuse my attire. I didn't know we were going to have company. Why didn't anyone tell me we were going to have company, Ben? Especially, company that just barges in your room when you're stark naked." Ms. Susie looks over at Beta and Beta smiles back.

"Mrs. Brackett is this tall, dark handsome man your driver?"

"No Miss Susie, this tall, dark and handsome man is my husband, John."

"He reminds me of my Rudy, so much." She cries.

"Ben, I think you need to get Ms. Susie back to her room." Nakdi said. After Susie left, I puff a sigh of relief.

"Ms. Susie's brain is stuck back to when we were living in South Carolina. The Rudy she mentioned is Nigel's father. It still amazes me she fell in love with Rudy."

Mrs. Brackett sat down. "This is a lot to take in."

"I know Mrs. Brackett." I said.

"You all call me Susan and my husband's name is John."

"Susan and John. This is my best friend Beta and her husband Henry."

Ben came back into the room and poured himself a scotch and offered John and Henry one as well. They all stood and downed the drinks and then sat back down.

"Nigel has always sensed he was different, that his story would someday be written in a book for everyone to read. He is brilliant. Growing up and even now as a young man. I want to tell him the truth, but not at this moment. I need to digest this myself. Deep down, I always knew I would have to tell him as much as I knew about his story."

"Susan, you both take all the time you need and when you are ready, we will be here to help and answer questions he may have. I know they are out there wondering if we have given our blessing."

Susan spoke, "Today, the Brackett's and the Henderson's will celebrate their union and next week we will come back out and tell them everything."

"Susan, we aren't going anywhere. When you're ready, let, us know."

"Okay, let me fix myself up and we can bring the children back in."

I took her to the washroom so she could freshen up. I went to Ben to hug him and for him to assure me we were doing the right thing by Nigel and Susie. For the time being, we were to act like nothing was out of sorts.

# 9

# The Truth About the Weaving Baskets

In the cool of the day, George, Nigel, and Maye rode back with Nigel's parents to their home. We had bid them a goodbye, and I hugged her with meaning. It wasn't more than an hour that passed before we heard George and Maye coming through the door. I went to Maye to express how everything progressed successfully, and we would have Nigel's parents over again soon.

Maye looked at me as though she perceived something was going on, but not the facts. My non-expression of being in another place than with her is what worried her most.

"Mom is everything alright?"

"Yes, love. Everything is fine. No matter what, know we love you so much and I am always here to love you and support you through any and everything that goes on in your life."

"I love you too, mother. Can I ask a question and get a straightforward answer?"

"Sure, my baby."

"Do you and father like Nigel?"

Nakdi smiled, because if that was all she wanted to know, this would be an easy one. "Maye, your father, and I truly like Nigel.

He's intelligent and very respectful of you, which is most important to us. One day when your children come home with their first boyfriend or girlfriend, you will understand all we want is what's best. In wanting that, we must allow you to find your way in life. Our people have fought hard and long to get where we are and to be free to love. Our lives are in danger every single day, but when love brings two people together, it's worth the fight and the risks. You are a young woman now. Find what's best for you. I'm sure your brothers will someday as well. George was a bit of a late bloomer, like his father. No worries, okay." All I could do was keep hugging her. Our environment exposed her to bigotry, but we tried to shield our children as much as possible. But the reality was life would bring it up close and personal to them all. She was old enough now to be out in the world and we wouldn't be there to fight her battles, especially in the love department, she would have to experience those for herself. I had sent Maye off with love.

I sat down in the living area with all the festering thoughts of the day. I heard Ben come into the room, watching me. Ben sat across from me in the chair. "I love you, Nakdi." My eyes glanced up at his and all I could do was smile.

"God has blessed us, Ben. Our children have survived some atrocities and the dreadful circumstances of our past and what we had to endure. Hate still abounds around us, because of the color of our skin. I sit here unashamed of who I am or falling in love with you. I sit here in the presence of a genuine man who could love me back despite the traditions of his history and the prejudices of bigotry. Out there in the world is not the same as in here. One day, our sons could hang from a tree, because of what they look like. We can't keep them hidden forever. We can't keep them from being hurt because of the world. It's everywhere and we should do our best to show them and be truthful with them. We have to teach them how to pick who they can trust on both sides of the fence. Teach them the reality of the true world we live in."

After the realization, they could kill my children one day. I cried. Susie came in twice to see if I was alright. I had Ben and Beta to comfort me, but my heart wasn't comforted.

~

"Nana, what was going on with you?"

"I think it saddened me at the fact there was a significant possibility my children would not make it to the age I am now. Life and death were in God's hands, and I realized we were not in control of their destiny. It took me two days to get over my anger with God and to release my anger at Ben for being white. I was angry at him for loving me and me loving him and us having children together. Wanting children badly, we didn't realize the repercussions of our decisions. Releasing the hatred, I had held onto since my childhood at the village elders and my parents that allowed me to be taken. I had to release the anger of Ms. Susie being in my home. I had to free my anger at God for creating me as I was, being taken and transported to a place against my will. Letting go of the evidence that even if I had joined with another African man, my children would nevertheless be in the probability of dying or taken to a farm and I would never see them again. I had to surrender the animosity that one day I would disappear and wouldn't be there to shield my children from our ghost past."

~

Looking at my Nana, I couldn't indeed express what I could understand in her. I had to leave.

"Nana, I'm going to go now. I will come back tomorrow."

"My dearest Nakida, I will see you tomorrow."

My Nana's body language adjusted to sadness as she was told this part of the story. I didn't know what to say to her or to know whether if anything I said would have made her feel any better. I hugged her and then left. All I could do was imagine the bitterness of knowing you lived through so much, but your children may not. I had thought little about God since Nana had mentioned Him in explaining her story. Growing up in church, I never thought about

Him in the context of controlling life and death in the way she thought about it back then. I wondered how she made it without going crazy like Ms. Susie. I guess we would get to that part soon enough.

~

I tried to forget about Nigel, Rudy, and Ms. Susie for a while, but got a visit from Susan Brackett the following week at the store. It pained her, but she wanted Nigel to know the truth. She had all kinds of questions for me I was willing to answer.

"How much does she remember?"

"Her memory of the past comes and goes. She is in the past most of the time and doesn't stay in the present too long. When Ben brought her to our home, she thought I was still a slave in service. We told her I was married to Ben when she arrived, but she doesn't remember half the time. She still thinks she's married to him. She speaks of a baby, but she doesn't know if it was a boy or a girl, if that makes any sense. If we put a child in her arms right this moment, she would think it was hers. She's been this way since the war, and she never returned to the reality of who she is now."

Ben walked into the front of the store and greeted Mrs. Brackett. "I guess you have decided?" he asked.

"Yes, I have. I want Nigel to know the truth of who he is and where he comes from. I was hoping all of us could be together and he can meet her."

"I'm sure with all the love and support we can offer. Everything will be just fine." I told her.

"I wanted to thank you both again for your hospitality on last week. If it's okay, I would like to do it this coming Saturday."

As Nakdi was about to answer, Maye had been standing by the storage door and heard them talking. "What do you need to tell Nigel?" Everyone shut down instantly, but they couldn't hide the fact they were talking about Nigel. "Mrs. Brackett, what are you doing here, is Nigel alright?"

I walked over to Maye and put my hands on her shoulders. Mrs. Bracket walked toward the front door. I looked back at her. "Don't worry, we will discuss this with Maye and explain everything." Ben walked Mrs. Brackett to her carriage.

Mrs. Bracket was charming in her own right. She had not aged badly like some others I had encountered. Soft and encouraging. Her Brunette hair was always rolled down to the middle of her back and she walked with grace. She hadn't been like the other ghosts. She was made from a different DNA.

"Mother, what is going on?" Maye asked.

"Maye, I need you to calm your nerves and sit down. I'm waiting for your father to return, so we can explain this to you together." Maye cries profusely. She had no clue what was going on and she just assumed she and Nigel wouldn't be seeing each other anymore.

"Mother, I thought you and father liked Nigel?"

"Maye, we do like Nigel. This has nothing to do with your relationship with him."

"Then why all the secrecy?"

"Maye, please just wait for your father to return, so we can discuss this together."

Maye was visibly shaking and now Nakdi was even more nervous and walked to the front of the store to see if Ben was coming back in. As Ben walked through the door, Maye turned to her father. "Father, what is going on? Why was Mrs. Brackett here?"

Ben stood next to Maye to explain everything. She sat intently while she heard the words, "Ms. Susie is Nigel's mother."

"Nigel is going to be so upset. He's had no clue all this time Mrs. Brackett was not his mother."

"Maye, Mr. & Mrs. Brackett want to tell Nigel themselves at our home on Saturday, so, you can't say anything to him about this. She wants him to know the truth, and she needs all the support she can get. So, I need you to promise me you won't say anything."

"I promise I won't say anything. Does George know anything about this?"

"No, he knows nothing yet."

"I won't see Nigel until Saturday anyhow, so, I won't be able to say anything. I just can't believe Ms. Susie is Nigel's actual mother."

"Well, she wasn't always touched in the head. I'll just leave it at that." I walked close to Maye.

"We're going to be leaving soon. When you get home, I want you to go rest yourself and I'll get you when supper's ready."

It was out in the open partially and I didn't know how Nigel was going to react to the news. Not only about Mrs. Brackett not being his biological mother, but the fact his biological mother was out of her mind. When we arrived home, Maye headed to her room, and I headed to the sitting room and looked out into the depths of the fields growing. Ben came behind me and just held me.

"You know our children don't know the whole truth. I don't want to tell them all the horrid details of the war and how we had to leave the farm. I just want to get through this Saturday and move on with our lives."

Ben turned me around. "Nakdi, we should discuss our lives with them some time. They need to know who they are and where they come from and the truth about the plantation and the truth about who we are as individuals."

"Ben, if we tell them everything and I mean everything, how do you think that's going to change their perspective of you and where we come from?"

"Nakdi, I am not regretful of who I've grown into. The man I've become is not that twenty-one-year-old who put you on the boat and did everything he could to please his father, even pretend to be like him, just to get him to like or love me. I want them to know the truth, because I never want my actions to be justified, but I want them to learn that people can change and truly stand up for what is good and true in the world. If I could reverse any of it and still meet you, I would do it in a heartbeat. Telling our children, the whole horrible truth will be a learning opportunity for them to know that bad and ugly things happen to good people. They need to know all the white people who exist in this world are not all evil. They need to know where you were born and come from is a beautiful place, they can be proud of. Telling them the truth will allow them to be clear of the bitterness they hear from others and, to a certain extent, they've never had to experience firsthand the inhumanity of those before them had to experience and our hope is the mindset which exists will change. We have made baby steps in our humanity, but we certainly have a long way to go."

"I know, but I want Samuel to be old enough to understand. Ben, I trust our love, it's out there I don't trust, and you can't fault me for living and seeing the ugly truth of where we are as a human race, but I know they have to know the truth, just like Nigel must know his truth as well."

Just as Nakdi finished, Samuel ran in to show them his progress report.

"Father, mother, here is my report. I trust you will be pleased."

"Ahh! Someone's sixteenth birthday is coming up. What are we doing for you this year?"

"I would like to have a party with a few of my friends, if that's alright?"

Nakdi looked over at Ben and then back at Samuel. "How about we sit down on Sunday afternoon and hash out the details?"

"That sounds great, if you are not saying no, I'm happy." Samuel thanked them both and then walked out of the sitting area as happy as one boy could get.

"Yes, they have truly been sheltered too much from reality." They both laugh, but knew it was serious.

I had always known that Ben's money kept us from a certain level of cruelty. I was no longer someone's property, and those who came into the store knew it. The ghosts would often put on airs, whether they had money or not. It was their mindset that their superiority didn't change if they had money, but I was called many things that Ben's money could not shield me from.

Saturday came, and rightfully so. There was still an uneasy feeling in the air. Ben was up earlier than usual on the farm with Franklin, and I had been up an hour earlier than he had been preparing breakfast. I made coffee like I had every morning, but this time, I sat outside on the porch and watched the sun come up for the first time in twenty years. I was now graying and wondered if I would live much longer. I had loved, and I had hated, I was once bitter and now I could forgive. I had seen hatred toward my people and that part had changed little. I had trusted and was betrayed. I had lied and told the truth. I had experienced loss and gained on the battlefield of my life. I experienced living during those years in Vieux Carre'.

~

"Nana, whatever happened with Nigel?"

"Oh, Nigel was happy to know the truth about where he came from, but he could never call her mother as she never raised him. I think he was a little upset at the fact he wasn't told sooner, but that quickly went away. After the millions of questions, he had for Ben and me, your great-uncle Nigel married your aunt Maye two years later. Your uncle George died of pneumonia at thirty-two and never married. He did go on to graduate with honors and wanted to become an inventor. Maye and Nigel had three children and stayed in Vieux Carre' and never left. Your grandfather Samuel married Abigail Simms, after he finished college and they moved to Chicago where he began teaching English."

"So, Nana, why did you leave Louisiana?"

"At sixty-three, your great-grandfather died of the cancer. He left me everything he owned, including the farm in South Carolina. After Ben died, there was no more holding on to the past. I left Ms. Susie in the care of Nigel and Maye, and I wanted to travel the world. I sold everything that could be sold, except the Henderson Plantation to tear it down. Once I tore down the house in South

Carolina, I built houses on the land and farm and rented them to African people who were displaced during that time. I deeded the house over to Maye and Nigel in Vieux Carre'. I did just what I set out to do. At 60, I had over a million dollars at my disposal, which was unheard of back then for a black woman. Of course, I paid for everyone's education, as I am paying for you."

"Nana, after great grandpa died, and you had all the money, did people treat you different?"

"In some circles, they did, but I still had to be careful. I traveled back to Africa the first chance I got to see if any of my family was still alive. There were a few cousins who remembered me because of my height, and I could see where my parents were laid to rest. My brother and sister were long gone, and no one knew where they lived now. I left there crying and aware of whom I had become, because of the circumstances of my destiny. I treasure every bit of my life. It certainly could have turned out differently. I hope and pray one day your generation finds the freedom and peace you deserve among this nation. I know I will never live to see it come to pass."

~

In 1942, my great-grand mother Nakdi Okuda-Henderson died of old age at 106. Leaving behind my great-aunt Maye at 74 years of age and my grandpa Samuel, 70 years of age. My great-aunt Maye had four children: William, Eliza, Nigel Jr. and Benjamin II. My grandpa Samuel had three children, Patricia, Sheldon, and George II, which I am the daughter of Sheldon and Mary Henderson. Nakdi's legacy (my great-grandmother's legacy) and the legacy of all others like her will continue to live on as we (their children of the cause) continue to tell the stories of their heroic lives and go beyond the color of love, no matter the obstacles of *The Ghosts of Slaveries Dance*. There're no more chains holding me.

The End

# *About the Author*

The passion to write for A. R. Leonard, started in High School, where an English Teacher, Mr. Katzman, encouraged folly, fun learning, and the joys of literature. In her early twenties, having vivid dreams, *Amethyst Love* (Amazon, 2019, Rev. 2025) and *Mercy Undercover* (Lulu,2025) were born. There were many dreams that followed, which spawned other books, such as *Unconditional Counsel* (CFP, 2020, Lulu.com, Rev. 2025). *Apocalyptic 7-Salvations Cry (Lulu.com, 2021, Rev. 2025),* birthed from a dream during her writing *Unconditional Counsel.* Current projects for *Embrace the Dawn to Live Again* (Amazon, 2024) and future Works in Progress are, *Unconditional Counsel 2: Fate Unbroken, Apocalyptic 8-Angels of Heaven's Armies, The Container, Opposing Fruit, and The Heart of an Untold Legacy: A Father's Story.*

In 2016, she created Nita Nae's Books to fuel the imagination of readers. In 2014, encouraged to start publishing her books, she is now paying it forward by helping others realize their dream of writing and completing books, which include, *Breakthrough to Visions Destiny* (LaWanda Jackson), *God Created You for Greatness* (Yakyshia Hooks) and *Embrace the Dawn: To Live Again* (Margo E. Leonard, mother), *My American Dream* (Yaba), *Magi Baba: A Magical Holiday Adventure* (Sandra Kinji), *Love is So Cool* (Clint D. Johnson), *God Kept Me* (Stephanie Johnson), *The Last Lady Standing in Ujima Village* (Navaline Smith), *Child of Addiction* (Patrice Smith), *Nothing To It But To Do It!* (Arlice Marshall).

Visit: www.nitanaesbooks.com to order your autographed copy.

E-mail (s):
nitanaes_books@yahoo.com or arnitarllewis@nitanaesbooks.com.

Follow Me on Social Media:
FB: nitanaesbooks
IG: nitanaesbooks
Twitter: NitaNaesBooks
Pinterest: nitanaesbooks

For Author interviews and book information:

NNB Author's Point of View Blog & YouTube Channel
NNB Author's P.O.V. BLOG | nitanaesbooks.com and
YouTube Channel https://youtu.be/OePi-LCJz_A

# Research References

Source:
http://www.historyworld.net/wrldhis/PlainTextHistories.asp?historyid=ac64#ixzz3eu9CpMf2

Source:
http://www.chocolatecity.cc/2014/07/06/the-devils-punchbowl-a-u-s-concentration-camp-for-black-slaves/

- Authors: P. Scott Corbett, Volker Janssen, John M. Lund, Todd Pfannestiel, Sylvie Waskiewicz, Paul Vickery
- Publisher/website: OpenStax
- Book title: U.S. History
- Publication date: Dec 30, 2014
- Location: Houston, Texas
- Book URL: https://openstax.org/books/us-history/pages/1-introduction
- Section URL: https://openstax.org/books/us-history/pages/16-2-congress-and-the-remaking-of-the-south-1865-1866